GAME, SET & LOVE MATCH

By Maggi Heath

First published in Great Britain by CGE Publishing Ltd

ISBN: 978-909061-11-8

Printed and bound by
Good News Books Ltd, Ongar, Essex, England.

For Ruff –
who thought
this was possible
and is always an
inspiration.

CHAPTER 1

'Oh, no.'

Gabriella, one foot balanced on the side of the bath, surveyed the nail polish which had slightly missed her middle toenail. Removing the stray blob of "Dark Velvet Rose," she concentrated again.

'Not very good at this.'

The trouble was, the big toe was fairly easy and then it got harder as the nails got smaller. Steadying her hand, she did another. Now only the

...

'Damn and Blast.'

Her phone was ringing and she slipped the tiny brush back into the bottle and ran, while trying to keep her toes splayed, into the bedroom. Retrieving her mobile and flopping onto the bed, she recognised her boss's number.

'Hi Steve. How're you?'

'Gabriella, sorry to ring on a Sunday, but we've got a bit of a family crisis.'

'Oh, no. A serious one?'

Steve, his wife Julie and their two young children didn't often have dramas in their lives, so she hoped it wasn't anything too disastrous.

'No. No. Julie's just come off her bike this afternoon and sprained her ankle. She won't be able to drive for a bit, so I'll have to do the school-run.'

'Oh right. Painful but could have been worse. OK I'll tell the staff to expect you when they see you.'

There was a slight pause.

'Ah, but you've forgotten what I was supposed to be doing this week.'

Her memory kicked in.

'Oh gosh, yes – that Conference in London.'

'So, my second reason for ringing, so you can have a bit of time to think about it, is to ask if you want to go in my place. Three days, Tuesday to Thursday but it's not residential, you'd just have to travel.'

'And would you like me to go instead of you?'

'Might as well, if you want to. It may not be very interesting, but it's good to hear what other firms are up to and what the latest HR buzzwords are.'

Gabriella chuckled.

'Didn't think we were particularly into buzzwords.'

'We're not. But at least we'll recognise them if other people start using them. Listen, think about it and let me know tomorrow – I'll bring in my Info Pack and the train tickets in case you decide to go.'

Sending love to Julie and promising to have an answer by tomorrow, she put her phone down and was about to start drying her hair when she noticed a naked toenail.

Driving into work, Gabriella felt pretty upbeat for a Monday. She had decided to go to the Conference and was looking forward to the three days out of office. She enjoyed work but it would be different and maybe there would be a chance to do a bit of shopping in the lunch hour. So, once in the office she was ready to get down to work, sort out anything urgent and tell Alex, Tani and Fay that Steve would be in later. Having accomplished the latter, she set-to.

'Morning.'

It was quarter past nine and Steve was standing in the doorway.

'Manic, that school-run, absolutely manic. You women, totally ferocious at eight-thirty in the morning behind the wheel of a car.'

Gabriella laughed.

'Exactly why I don't do that sort of thing.'

Steve grinned at her.

'Yes, Julie and I were discussing that after I'd rung you.'

The grin was turning vulpine.

'Time you got yourself sorted out with a good chap, you know.'

'Really? And where do you find these "good chaps"? I don't seem to locate them on my supermarket shelves or standing around with a little placard saying "Good chap in need of a good home."'

They'd done this sort of verbal sparring over her single status before – lots of times.

'Ah, well. I'll tell you where you might strike lucky. Oh, by the way, are you going to that Conference instead of me?'

She nodded.

'Good, well, just the place to encounter Mr Right, I should think.'

Now Gabriella's grin was widening.

'Really? Why's that for heaven's sake? Thought it was a Human Resources Conference not a Singles bash.'

'Well a man has to be regarded as a Human Resource, so as I said, you just might strike lucky. Who knows?'

'Who knows indeed? And I do promise I'll keep a lookout. Just for you. I know how you have my best interests at heart. Now, cut all this rubbish and give me the Info Pack, please.'

Running later than she intended on Tuesday morning, she drove into the station car park. Pulling on the brake and lurching out of the car she looked for the nearest ticket-machine. Why were they always up the other end from where you'd parked? She started towards the machine, trying to locate her purse and realising that the pencil skirt and high heels she had chosen were not the best for hurrying over the potholes. Shouldn't have gone for the power-dressing, but too late now. Remember for tomorrow.

Even this early in the morning, the platform was packed and she wasn't sure where to stand for the best. Although she sometimes caught the train to work in Cadmore on days she didn't drive, she was rarely on the station platform at this time. But, as the London-bound train pulled in, she found herself in a group who all seemed to surge towards one door and it was a good move as there were a few seats in the compartment. She looked round at the commuters already on the train, some fast asleep, some working, some plugged in to music and marvelled that they had the stamina to do this every day. Settling back, she closed her eyes.

At Waterloo, she decided on a taxi to the Conference hotel. The distance was easily walkable in the time, unless you were the wearer of high-heels and a pencil skirt. Dropped outside, she took a deep breath, checked in with reception, found the room and, smiling to cover any latent nerves, pushed open the door.

The morning session had been mind-numbingly boring; two guest speakers, neither of whom managed fully to grab her attention and going over pretty old stuff, she thought. Definitely no buzzwords on offer. So when the course broke for lunch, Gabriella hoped there would be chance to escape to the shops.

'Now, delegates.'

Colin, one of the two facilitators, was holding up a hand for their attention.

'The hotel has provided a buffet lunch set out in the anteroom and we will be coming round while you eat to tell you your groups for the discussion sessions this afternoon.' Gabriella groaned inwardly. Bang goes the shopping.

'Coming through, Gabriella?'

She turned and had recognised the voice. Tall, thin, bald and already marked down as very boring from the incessant questions he had posed during the morning session, she was in no mood for Clive or Keith or whatever his name was. "Strike it lucky?" Oh, no, no, no.

'Not quite. Have to find the cloakroom,' she noted a flash of embarrassment crossing his face, 'and then do a few calls and messages.'

Smiling, she headed for the door and hoped she would turn in the right direction for the Ladies. The cloakroom was delightfully luxurious and Gabriella started to entertain fantasies of staying there all afternoon. However, these thoughts were ended by the arrival of another course member, an older woman whose name she couldn't remember and they started to chat. Introductions were made and in the safety of a new-found friendship Gabriella and Marina headed for lunch, both agreeing that at least a discussion group might enliven the tedium – but only might.

Fortunately, Gabriella's group was reasonably lively and she had fun countering some outrageous views being put forward by an extremely young-looking man called Brendan. He was either very naïve or doing it tongue-in-cheek because he too was bored. Somehow, she thought it was the former. And after that session, tea and the wash-up, they had got to the end of Day One with handouts and exhortations to be on time for an exciting day tomorrow. Hailing a cab, she knew she would be glad to get home. In fact, if things didn't improve, she would be glad to get back to work on Friday.

Hurrying as much as she could onto the station concourse with five minutes to spare before the five-twenty-five's departure, and approaching the platform barrier, she heard the distorted tones of the announcer apologising for the cancellation of the five-twenty-five train due to a lack of drivers. That was irritating, but it just seemed to be in keeping with how this day had been going. However, it was a half-hourly service in the rush hour and the buffet, although not totally inviting, would at least provide a coffee to while away twenty minutes or so. She queued behind several other commuters who had evidently had the same idea before purchasing her coffee and edging towards a small table, carrying the rigid cardboard carton of cappuccino (or the station's idea of what they thought cappuccino should be). Setting it down, she sank onto the hard, plastic chair.

'The destination of the totally trapped.'

The voice came from the next table. She looked across. A dark-haired young man, about her own age, dressed in the usual commuter's suit and smart shirt, was smiling at her.

'If you're in the buffet, it means that you have nowhere else to go until the railway decides to take you away – so you're trapped by them until that moment. Are you a victim of the cancelled five-twenty-five?'

Gabriella was amused by his smiling cynicism.

'Yes. But I don't feel too trapped actually. I'm looking on it as an opportunity to have an extra coffee.'

'Ah, a beautiful face and a sunny nature. By the way, my name's Mark. Who are you? I don't think I have seen you on the train before.'

'Gabriella. And I don't often use the train.'

Making a determined effort to disengage eye contact and drink some of the coffee, she didn't really want to get into a prolonged conversation. All she wanted was to get home as quickly as possible. She had managed about half of the coffee when the announcer broke into another garbled message which she could barely hear, but thought it might be something about the five-fifty-five service.

'Come on. Quick.'

Mark, clutching his briefcase from the chair, was starting for the door.

'Come on. Got to beat the rush to the seats.'

He obviously intended her to follow and as he seemed to know what he was doing, she picked up her handbag, left the coffee and stumbled out of the buffet with him.

'Front of the train,' he shouted over his shoulder, 'more seats there when it's packed like it will be tonight.'

He was walking very rapidly past the line of carriages; Gabriella, feet hurting like hell and hobbled by the skirt, was unable to keep up. But she saw him as he eventually disappeared into a carriage near the front of the train shouting for her to follow. Trying to hurry, she boarded at last and found him guarding two seats in an end compartment. She collapsed into one and took a few minutes catching her breath. Commuters were now streaming through the compartment in both directions, pushing against each other and gradually becoming resigned to the fact that the train was full – very full.

'You seem to have this commuting down to a fine art. I don't, so I'm grateful for you grabbing the seats. Thanks.'

Once the train had pulled out of the station and the crush of travellers without seats had eased around them, she hoped she might be able to close her eyes and doze for a little. It turned out that there was no chance of that as Mark wanted to talk and it seemed churlish not to respond. She had to explain about the Conference, which was not a usual part of her daily travelling routine and then he wanted to know whether she had a car. When she'd told him about the yellow convertible she drove, he wanted to know how she decided, on normal workdays, whether to drive or go by train. She had to confess that there was no logic involved, it was decided on a whim or might be influenced by weather or shopping needs. He asked about the kind of work she did and how long she had been there and told her that he was in the media business in reply to one of the few questions Gabriella managed to ask.

'Where are you getting off?'

She told him that her stop was Upton Peploe.

'I go a couple of stops further on,' he replied, 'but tonight, I think I'll get off the train with you and take you out for a drink.'

Gabriella was totally taken aback by this but decided that firm politeness would be sufficient to put him off.

'I'm sorry, that won't be possible. I've already got plans for the evening.'

Bit of a white lie.

'And the cancellation has already made a tight schedule even tighter. Thank you, but I can't accept.'

He seemed to weigh up whether this was an excuse or not.

'How about a very quick drink and you can say you're late because the train was cancelled? That's the truth isn't it?'

She smiled, but was getting irritated with his persistence.

'I'm sorry, the answer is no.'

The train was slowing and nearing the station and Gabriella stood, wondering what she would do if he decided to get off as well.

'OK. Lovely Gabriella. I'll let you go this time, but I'm sure we shall meet again and have that drink. Here, this is my card.'

She took the proffered card, nodded an acknowledgement and walked down the compartment to where other commuters were queuing by the door. He made no move to follow her and she didn't look into the carriage as she walked past and down the platform to the exit and the car park. As she walked, she glanced at the card he had given her.

MARK HADDON

Media Consultant

Whizz Productions Inc

Not bothering to read the address or telephone numbers, she threw it in the bin.

'Forward and brash,' she muttered as she neared the spot in the car park where her little convertible was standing.

On Wednesday, as she drove into the station she was a touch apprehensive. Not wishing to see Mark Haddon again, she hoped that he wasn't on such an early train. But she would be circumspect and try to avoid him at all costs. Recognising a couple of the men who had been there yesterday talking earnestly, she stood behind them, using them as a human shield. This really is a bit stupid, she thought, but all was well as the train was approaching. Then all turned out not so well as there were no seats. Ah well, at least the flat ballet-pumps today will help.

'Good morning all. Now today we are going to tackle one of the perennial knotty problems in HR – Industrial Tribunals. I'm afraid you've got me first and then we're really lucky to have Suzanne Balletone with us from "The Priceless People Bureau."'

Gabriella tried not to grin openly as she thought "priceless people" could be taken as a bit of a double entendre. But Colin, the facilitator, was looking eager to begin expounding and Gabriella picked up a pencil ready to do some notes, feeling that she ought to give this her best attention. After half an hour, looking round the horseshoe table while more handouts were being distributed, she was horrified to see

Clive/Keith smiling at her, mouthing "Hello" and giving a little wave. Managing to keep her expression entirely un-altered, she ignored him and engaged the man next to her in conversation while they sorted out these new pieces of paper. What had Steve said about meeting "Mr Right"? Well neither Mark Haddon nor Clive/Keith could remotely be placed in that category. Roll on lunch-time.

Day Two finally juddered to an end, having been temporarily enlivened by Suzanne who had been interesting and eccentrically dressed in a tuxedo jacket and jeans. As she was collecting her things together she became aware of a lurking presence behind her.

'Gabriella.'

The face was glowing, the bald head shining and Clive/Keith was barring her way to the door.

'A few of us are going for a drink, having a little bonding session,' he laughed and threw his hands up in what seemed an almost camp gesture.

'You must come so we can all get to know each other, do a bit of networking and all that. Going to do it today as people will be rushing off tomorrow.'

'Oh, how kind. Lovely idea but I'm afraid I'm rushing off today, so really can't join you. Shame but there it is.'

And she bolted past him, hearing him offer up a lame-sounding, 'Bye – till tomorrow then,' as she went.

Glancing at her watch she calculated there was time to walk to the station and just make the five-twenty-five. Please let it be running, though there was no way she would tackle the station buffet again. Reaching the concourse she got through the barrier and onto the last carriage of the train. Good, on two counts: she'd made it and she could see that there was no Media Consultant occupying any of the seats. Settling back as the train pulled out, she relaxed, the memory of

Clive/Keith's abject expression as she had turned down the "bonding session" floating across her mind. Thank goodness there was only one more day of this. Jolted awake and surprised that she had slept, the train was pulling into Cadmore, the stop before hers. Ten more minutes and then home, a meal, a bit of easy-watching TV, shower and bed. Glancing out of the window, watching the patchwork of fields, the woods and occasional buildings she jumped as the voice broke across her quiet moment.

'Found you at last.'

Mark Haddon was smiling down at her.

'Hello. Didn't know you had been looking for me.'

She hoped her tone was suitably dismissive and started to gather her bag and folder of handouts.

'Oh, but I was. Remember I said we'd have that drink. Well, it's tonight. So where shall we go? You know the area.'

She was stunned by his arrogance.

'Sorry. No drink, Mark.'

Getting out of her seat as the train started to slow, she walked the length of the carriage to the far exit. Gratefully, others who were getting off filed in behind and although she gave a quick glance round, Mark Haddon was not among them. The doors opened but nothing happened. Standing, a bit anxious about the delay, she realised that a very elderly gentleman with two walking sticks was being helped off. Finally the rest of their group disembarked and she walked steadily for the exit. But her heart was thumping. Suppose he had been fool enough to get off? Crossing the car park, she kept close to a couple who had evidently been shopping and when she got to the rubbish bin, stopped suddenly, turned and looked behind. Not there. Breathing a little easier, she reached her car and got in. Joining the queue, she was exiting the car park when she looked right as she passed the taxi rank just in time to see Mark Haddon getting into one and, as she took another glance in the rear-view mirror, saw the distinctive yellow-and-black taxi slot in three cars behind hers. Heart pumping more wildly, imagination in overdrive, she started to feel scared. They were going slowly through the town and in her anxiety to keep glancing back she nearly pranged the car in front. Taking the familiar route, her mind was now racing, panicking. What was she going to do? Damn and blast you, Mark Haddon. If she drove to the police station, he would simply drive on. If she stopped somewhere, he would stop and wait. The one thing she couldn't do, as the lights changed and she shot erratically forward, was to go home. But soon she would need to do something. The fuel gauge was registering over half a tank and she remembered his words, "You know the area." Suddenly she knew exactly what to do and turned north at the next junction, heading for the outskirts of town. The taxi was still there, now two cars behind.

'Right, Mr Haddon,' she had no idea why she was shouting, but fear and outrage had got the adrenalin flowing, 'let's take you on a nice long drive and see how far you want to go by expensive taxi.'

When the sign for "M36 Motorway - 2 miles" came up, she actually laughed.

'Nice evening for a drive, Mr. Haddon.'

If she had to drive all the way down the motorway to her friend's house, she didn't care. Turning off onto the slip road, her view was blocked by a huge lorry coming up behind her, but once on the motorway, looking back, there was no taxi in sight. Relaxing her grip on the steering wheel, she drove on, occasionally checking there was no following taxi, until she came to the slip road which meant she could cross to the other side of the motorway and return home.

Getting into bed that night, she was still furious about what had happened, but pleased that she had managed to outwit him. Now there was tomorrow to negotiate and she set the alarm forty minutes earlier.

'Morning Gabriella, you're an early-bird. That's the sort of commitment we like to see from delegates.'

Colin and Julie-Anne had entered the Conference Room and were clearly not expecting Gabriella to be already there. Muttering something about needing to catch a different train (getting the seven-fifteen had been worth the early start) she asked about the structure of the day, explaining that she really needed to be away a little earlier that afternoon.

'Not a problem.'

Julie-Anne was smiling her professional, "we can deal with any difficulty," smile.

'We always halve the lunch break on the last day and aim to finish by four at the latest. Will that be alright for you?'

'Perfectly, thanks.'

Colin was plugging in his laptop and looked up.

'How's the Conference been for you Gabriella? We do like to have feedback from our delegates.'

Ah. This could be tricky.

'Well I really wasn't sure what to expect, so it has all been a useful experience and I have learnt things in areas where my knowledge was a bit sketchy. So thank you both for sharing your expertise and time with us.'

She was aware that was the sort of congratulatory jargon which was frequently bandied about at the end of conferences or courses, but the two recipients of the accolade were obviously pleased.

Seven and a half hours to go.

At quarter to four it was obvious that the last information had been disseminated and digested, case studies had been dissected and there was only the final handout to be passed round. The two facilitators reminded them of the need to "Walk the Talk" and, having met each other, to keep networking. Gabriella nearly giggled out loud at that. But, saying her goodbyes, she even managed a courteous farewell to Cliff - she had finally registered that was his name - who was promising everyone he would be in touch. Now, to the station.

The earlier train was much less crowded and she selected a seat opposite a middle-aged couple. As she sank into that strange velveteen upholstery which seemed the default fabric for train seats these days, she sighed.

'London does that to you, doesn't it?'

The lady opposite was smiling.

'Yes, it does. Have you been shopping?'

The couple, eager to tell of their exploits, recounted their day's sightseeing and for once, the journey passed pleasantly and uneventfully. But tomorrow, she would have serious words with Steve about conferences and their usefulness and don't let him dare mention finding "Mr Right."

It was bliss to be home earlier than normal. There was an M&S meal in the fridge and only one working day before the weekend. Great.

When the phone rang, she half feared it was Cliff starting on his networking. No, not possible, she'd made very sure no-one had taken any personal details from her. Don't be paranoid. Picking up the phone, not remotely recognising the local number, she heard the once familiar, booming tones of George Bunting.

'Gabriella. Good evening to you. Hope this isn't a bad time,' he didn't wait to find out, 'but you contacted me several weeks ago about coming back to the tennis club. Now, time is getting on and as I believe you said you would re-join and annual subscriptions are now due, I thought I ought to give you a little nudge, figuratively speaking of course.'

George seemed to think that last bit extremely funny and while she waited for him to stop laughing, started to dredge up the commitment about joining she seemed to have given. Then George was off again.

'So I was ringing to see whether you would be down this weekend. I don't want you to miss too many weeks out of the year.'

'Well, George, I've been a bit busy this week, working in London and...'

'Oh, well, fresh air and exercise should be just the thing for you. We've got a good group of folks who come down on Fridays and Saturdays particularly, nice people, you'll enjoy meeting them.'

'Really? I mean yes, that sounds fine. But I can't promise it will be this weekend, because...'

She had no time to finish the excuse.

'Well, Alice is looking forward to seeing you again and I'm sure you'll enjoy it. So I'll expect to see you.'

And that seemed to be it.

When they had rung off, Gabriella sat in her chair and thought. Come on, it seems to be "make your mind up time" and "nice people" on offer. Was she going to do this? Well, if you aren't going to, what was the use of buying those new sports clothes and racket? Dishing up her meal, she thought about the pros and cons. Don't be so spineless. There aren't any cons. This isn't a difficult decision. Just do it. Picking up her knife and fork, she started to eat.

On Friday when she reached the office, she was surprised to see Steve's car already parked. Once at her desk, she sorted through the drift of Post It notes, expected there would be a huge number of emails to read and noted that Steve was seeing a client but would be free at eleven for a chat. When he sauntered in Gabriella knew she must try to be objective.

'So, how was it?'

Steve, plus coffee cup settled into the chair opposite her desk.

'First things first. How's Julie and why were you in early?'

He gulped some coffee and sat back.

'Much improved, so good in fact that I've given up the school-run.'

Gabriella looked at him.

'Too tough an assignment for a mere male?'

He nodded.

'Too true and speaking of which, or should that be whom?'

'Don't ask.'

He crowed with laughter.

'Ah, no "Mr Right" after all. Didn't really think there would be and what was the Conference like?'

'Not very inspiring, probably only just worth going to, so not a great experience - and I got stalked on the way home.'

'What?'

Steve had nearly spilt his coffee. She explained about Mark Haddon.

'What a bastard. You see, you do need a chap in your life, but...'

He threw up his hands in a gesture of surrender.

'OK, OK. I suppose you'll find the right one eventually. Anyway, thank you for going. Sorry it wasn't too good and as a treat, we're all leaving the office a bit early tonight.'

He rose and stopped at the door.

'Got any plans for the weekend?'

'Don't know yet. Think I might re-join the local tennis club. And...'

She fixed him with one of her not-to-be-messed-with looks.

'I'm going there to play tennis. Understood?'

CHAPTER 2

Gabriella closed the wardrobe door and turned to look in the mirror. She remained motionless, staring at her reflection for another fifteen seconds or so.

'Have to do,' she announced to the reflection, exited her bedroom, ran downstairs collecting handbag, keys and sports bag before locking up and walking purposefully out to her car. She threw her bag into the boot and settling into the driving seat, adjusted the visor and put on her sunglasses before pulling out into the road and heading off for Upton Peploe Lawn Tennis Club.

The Friday night traffic was snarled up as usual and she tapped her fingers on the steering wheel waiting for the queue to stop/start up to the lights. What on earth is that? She glanced irritably to her right to see, alongside her, a small black car, equally stationary on the other side of the road. Its occupant's head was nodding ferociously, hands banging the steering wheel in unison and a cacophonous boom, boom, boom, yeow, yeow, yeow, thudding through the frame of her car as well as his. She gave him a look and then realised that with sunglasses on he couldn't decipher her pitying stare.

Disliking his noise, she stopped the syncopation from her own fingers and watched the lights. Green. Green for Go. The queue eased forward and then the lights turned red again as she was approaching. I hope this isn't symptomatic of how the rest of the evening is going to be. She sat, waiting, realising that she was starting to have second thoughts about this, despite the fact that it had seemed a good idea last night. Oh, come on, get a grip she argued with her faltering resolve, you're a grown woman for goodness sake and this is hardly life-threatening stuff you're attempting.

At last, she was across the lights and making reasonable headway through the town. She knew the way to the club perfectly well, knew

George Bunting, who had been the Club Secretary and main organiser the last time she had been a member. Even remembered what his wife Alice looked like. But that was ten years ago. And just at this exact moment, ten years seemed like half a lifetime. She laughed at her ropey maths, well about a third of a lifetime, so long enough, absolutely long enough.

Accelerating through a gap in the oncoming traffic, she passed the turn into The Avenue (rather nice detached houses and tree-lined as its name suggested) and then took the next left which led onto Common Road and then the little lane where the club had its courts and pavilion. It had taken much longer than the expected six or seven minutes to reach the lane and turn in through what she noticed were new iron gates.

'Wow!'

She couldn't help the surprised exclamation. She had prepared herself, mentally, for the changes which George had briefly hinted at, but hadn't expected things to be so, well, so different. The car park had tarmac instead of hard core and grass and there seemed to be more courts than she remembered.

Parking and switching off the engine, she sat and surveyed the club where she had spent her teenage years. But what had it been like then? Despite trying to conjure up the atmosphere, the people, she found there were very few memories to go on. But somehow, she felt things were different, which was a stupid feeling if she honestly couldn't remember much about its original state. Perhaps anxiety had given her some sort of selective amnesia she thought wryly.

Looking through the windscreen again, she was sure of two things: the club was definitely bigger - four courts instead of just two - and the pavilion door, which had always been a shabby olive-green, was now deep blue.

'Well, well,' she murmured, 'better go and see what else is new.'

But she didn't move. Instead she took a deep breath, realising that this wasn't going to be the same; things had moved on, there would be different people whom she no longer knew and, horrible thought, her tennis was going to be pretty rusty as well. I think you're being a bit of a wimp an inner voice told her and, at its critical prompting, she swung her legs out of the car, retrieved her bag and walked towards the blue-painted doorway.

'Gabriella, good to see you.'

George had appeared in the doorway and at first she was shocked to see how he looked, he was grey, he was stouter. But then, she realised, he too was ten years older.

'Hi George, this place has changed a bit. I was expecting something different but not quite this – I thought you said the club had nearly folded a few years ago – it looks pretty thriving now.'

George almost visibly puffed out his chest with pride.

'Um, yes, well things did go through a sticky patch but we've managed to pull it round with a rescue plan I put forward.'

He leant towards her and held his hand over his mouth as though about to share a great secret.

'Lot of hard work of course,' he confided conspiratorially.

'I'm sure. But you always were a bit of a dab hand at getting things done, George, so right man for the job, I'd say.'

Gabriella smiled inwardly as she complimented him because in the old days George had always struck her as a bit self-important and she imagined that he really enjoyed running the show now. But, she had to admit, he seemed to have made a good enough job of it.

'Come on in and meet a few of the folks, you'll know Alice of course, but most of the others are new. They're generally a good crowd, so I'm sure you'll enjoy yourself. Alice,' he bellowed as he stepped back through the doorway, 'come and see who's arrived.'

George's wife emerged from a white-clad group and came forward with hands outstretched.

'So nice to have you back.'

'It's good to be back.'

They grasped each other by the shoulders and exchanged continental-style air kisses on both cheeks.

'Now,' George was not letting any further conversation develop, 'you may as well meet Tom while we're doing introductions, he's relatively new as well.'

Gabriella turned to where George was looking and saw that most of the group who had previously been chatting with Alice were making their way outside, leaving a tall, fair-haired man standing alone.

'This is Tom.'

George was looking at the younger man with a kind of reverent expression and Gabriella noted that he had lowered his normally booming voice.

'Tom is one of our best players, no he is our best player, though I doubt he will tell you so himself.'

The man whom George was introducing, dressed in immaculate tennis kit, was tall, athletically built and – Gabriella was almost transfixed – had the most amazing, deep blue eyes. She briefly wondered if he were Scandinavian.

'Tom, meet a...'

There was a loud crash from the far end of the pavilion where Gabriella remembered a small kitchen was situated.

'What the…'

George managed to stop the expletive but turned and scurried off to the kitchen, followed by a startled-looking Alice. Gabriella turned to face the club's best player, about to finish the introduction George had started, when he proffered a hand.

'Tom Scotford. Who are you? Are you new?'

She saw his gaze sweep from her head to her feet and then fix her with an enquiring, but cool, expression. She blinked, temporarily taken aback by the almost abrupt, peremptory tone of the questions. There was no warmth of greeting, nothing to put her at ease, just a bald request for information. Right she thought, yet another man who doesn't look as though he is going to be one of my all-time favourites. Ah well.

'Gabriella Devonshire.'

She shook his hand lightly and briefly, relinquishing his grip but looking challengingly straight into those amazing blue eyes. Her encounter with Mark Haddon had seemed to steel her responses and the next bit came out quickly and a bit more sharply than she had intended.

'And if the name is too long for you, then by all means shorten it to Gabriel, but never, ever, Gaby.'

She was a bit amazed at the riposte but, to her consternation, an amused smile spread across his face.

'I think I shall be able to manage Gabriella without too much trouble and I don't expect you will have any difficulty with Tom.'

He turned away just as George was returning.

'Ah you two have met. Good.'

He was back beside Gabriella.

'Bit of a crockery mishap. More expense.'

He gave a little laugh.

'Now, just excuse me while I see who has come and whether we can get you started with some tennis.'

Leaving her standing in the empty pavilion, he scurried outside where she heard him hailing some new arrivals and exhorting them to hurry up.

Left feeling very alone, Gabriella unzipped her sports bag and took out her new racket. She knew that people thought she was normally a confident person, but that wasn't always the case and just now, she was feeling nervous. She knew it was stupid, but her hands felt clammy and her mouth was dry. And so far, nothing had happened tonight to make her feel that coming back here had been a particularly good decision.

'At least I might look the part, if nothing else,' she muttered, trying to find comfort in the fact that her new sports clothes looked OK. She bent down and fiddled with her laces, although she knew they were fine, and secretly hoped that she wouldn't have to play with the Scotford man as there was something about him that was a bit unnerving. Twisting her racket in her hands, she suddenly heard George calling her name and bolted out of the pavilion, rather like a schoolgirl being summoned by the Head. Outside, George was standing with three other people, all about her age.

'Come on Gabriella, these folks have just arrived, so you can make up a four. Do the introductions yourselves,' he added as he left, making his way onto the courts where others were already waiting for him.

The woman in the group, dark curly hair and a wide-mouthed smile, stepped forward.

'Right, do as the man said.'

She let out a loud but cheery laugh.

'I'm Samantha, usually called Sam, this is my other half, Brian and this,' she was indicating the third in the group, 'is my young brother, Simon. You're Gabriella, yes?'

She gulped a mouthful of air.

'Yes. First visit tonight and not expecting to play very well, so hope you aren't too good.'

Sam let out a snorting laugh.

'No, no. We come here for a bit of fun and relaxation. Don't worry you'll be fine with us.'

Gabriella noted that Sam had been doing all the talking, but suddenly Simon spoke.

'OK Sam, you and your old man can play together and I and Gabriella will attempt to give you the run around.'

He looked at Gabriella questioningly.

'If that's alright of course?'

'Perfectly. But you'll need to do most of the running.'

They trouped onto the court, exchanging light banter and it was obvious that Sam was in charge, which suited Gabriella just fine. After a few minutes of knocking balls back and forth, Sam decreed they should play.

'Oooh. Hope this will be alright.'

Her confidence was ebbing again and Gabriella looked anxiously at Simon.

'Course it will, come on, give it a go.'

Simon was hitting balls up to the other end of the court but, she noticed, smiling encouragingly at her.

'It's only a game, have fun. I shall.'

So they started to play. Sam began serving and it wasn't long before Gabriella's worst fears were realised. She was dreadful. Racket and ball did occasionally connect, but it was by random chance rather than design and the net just seemed to be in the way and the court too narrow. The saving grace though was that the others weren't much better and, as Sam had predicted, they were treating it all as a game to be enjoyed, not a life or death contest. But the more they played, the more she relaxed and realised that, though her standard was abysmal, she was having fun.

'Wahay, look, I hit one.'

Such exultation over simply hitting the ball was really over the top but it was a warm, summer evening, she was getting some much needed exercise, these three people were friendly and she was also beginning to enjoy Simon's very laid-back style. In fact he was rather nice in an unassuming sort of way, gallantly scrambling round the court attempting to hit every ball which came in his direction and even some that didn't. Then, when he had missed one, he shouted, "Yours partner," and they dissolved into laughter. Concentrating hard, they were trying to capture one game, having lost the first three, when Gabriella hit a forehand drive. At least that was what she intended. For once her racket did connect well with the ball and she hit a stinging return, straight into the middle of Simon's back. Running up to him, full of anxiety, she felt such a fool.

'I'm so, so sorry, I didn't mean it.'

She was gazing into his face and biting her lip with embarrassment.

"S'alright, I'm fine. Really. Not hurt.'

They were standing very close together in the centre of the court, looking into each other's eyes.

'Well done, Gabriella, I often feel like clouting him one.'

Sam's remark broke the spell and they walked back to resume the game; but Gabriella had known there was something special about that moment.

'Concentrate, for goodness sake,' she hissed at herself and got ready to serve again.

Despite their combined efforts they lost and at the end she heard Simon saying that they would definitely have a re-match, as he was sure they had the beating of sister Sam and Brian. She smiled, breathing hard from the exertion, feeling a stitch in her right side gnawing relentlessly.

'I'm surprised you can put up with me, I've never played so badly in my life.'

She was so breathless she could hardly get the words out and leant on the net-post for a moment to recover. Hell, she didn't realise she was quite so unfit.

'So, we just need more practice,' he laughed as they walked off court, where George was hopping from one foot to the other.

'Simon, good, you've finished. Come and make up a four over on court three with Alice. Thanks.'

'Bye. See you a bit later, and we'll have a drink in the clubhouse.'

He sprinted off to join Alice and two others and Gabriella turned and walked back towards the pavilion. She was feeling, well she wasn't quite sure what, but was stopped from further emotional analysis by Sam skipping out from the doorway.

'Come on, I've got two others and we can have a ladies' four. You up for that?'

She was indeed.

The ladies' four was absolutely hilarious and Gabriella was having great fun, when in the middle of a game, after a particularly long rally, she suddenly heard a voice.

'Keep your head still and down longer on your forehand, you're bringing it up too soon.'

She wheeled round in amazement to see Tom Scotford casually watching her as he collected balls from the back of the courts. She gave him an absolutely thunderous look.

'Head still, remember.'

He gave her a little nod as if to emphasise that was what she must do and walked away. Gabriella bent down to pick up the ball which he had lobbed towards her, furious at this unexpected intervention. How dare he watch her in order to criticize her? For the next few minutes she was so angry she didn't have the sense to acknowledge that he was right. But once she had recovered some composure and the next time she had to hit a forehand, she could hear the words, tried to do it, and hit a winner.

'Hey, where did that come from?' yelled Sam.

'Don't quite know,' Gabriella yelled back, secretly rather pleased with herself just the same.

And the rest of the evening passed in a haze of introductions, some mediocre play, several definitely improving forehands and, she was delighted to note, a lot of really good fun. About nine the light was fading and most people were packing up or calling out goodbyes and as she came off the farthest court, Gabriella saw Simon outside the pavilion, watching her approach.

'Drink?'

'Er, yes. Good idea.'

She hadn't quite expected the evening to end on a social note, but realised that of all the people she had met, Simon was someone she would like to get to know a bit better. Liar, she told herself, she wanted to get to know him much better. At last things seemed to be shaping up a bit.

'Just let me put my bag in the car and I'll be right with you.'

As she walked back across the car park, she was beginning to experience quite a different sensation from the one on her initial walk into the pavilion. Anticipation? Recognition of something special? An important beginning? For someone who spent a lot of time at work analysing things, she was surprised to find herself at a loss with this one. But tonight she felt it was OK simply to go for it and see what would happen. Nothing ventured and all that.

The clubhouse, which had not even existed when she had previously been a member, was built behind a huge Leylandii hedge which screened it from the courts. They walked up the path and Simon pushed open the door. Facing them was an inner lobby and then swinging open another door, they entered a spacious lounge area with chairs and glass-topped tables and a bar at one end of a reasonably crowded room. Noisy, fractured conversations, laughter and the clink of glasses hit her as they entered. This was all new to her.

'What would you like?'

'Well, I'm a bit thirsty after that exercise and I'm driving, so I'd like an orange juice with sparkling water please.'

She waited, taking in the newness of the surroundings, wondering where all these extra people had come from, as they definitely weren't tennis players and acknowledging the fact that she was waiting to have a quiet drink with a very personable young man. Well, after the last few days, even on the law of averages, she was due an upturn in fortunes. Arriving with their drinks, Simon passed her a glass and then set off towards a table. She noted that it was at the far end of the room, in a corner, well away from the others who had come off court. They sat facing each other, suddenly both intent on drinking, suddenly both apparently tongue-tied. Gabriella, wondering how the conversation was going to start - but eager for things to get going - looked round at the crowd of drinkers.

'Do you know who all these people are? They haven't been playing tennis.'

'I think the club has a social as well as a playing membership. Sam said that they had the clubhouse built, which put the club into debt and then membership declined and things were a bit dicey. Then, George sort of stepped in, formed a board of trustees or something and more or less took over. Someone came up with the idea of offering a social membership and things took off again. At least I think that's what happened.'

Gabriella nodded, that would explain the bad patch which George had spoken about and the fact that he seemed to be more in charge than ever. Simon was looking at her expectantly and she suddenly realised he had asked her a question.

'Sorry, just thinking about the club's change in fortunes. What did you say?'

'Do you live and work in Upton Peploe'

'Yes and no. I live here but I work in Cadmore.'

'Doing what?'

'I'm a Human Resources Analyst.'

'And what does that mean?'

Gabriella was used to having to explain what that meant and gave him a quick rundown of the firm she worked for, set up by her boss, Steve, the three other staff and the type of HR projects which they undertook for firms who hadn't the expertise, resources or time to do the work themselves.

'Sounds interesting. Do you enjoy it?'

'Very much. Each day's different, some of the problems we get are challenging and interesting and you get a sense of achievement at helping others resolve things.'

Just as she finished speaking, there was a commotion around the bar area and Simon craned his head round to see what was happening.

'What's going on? Can you see?'

It sounded like some sort of argument was breaking out but while his attention was elsewhere Gabriella snatched a covert look at this young man opposite. A good imprint on her memory was needed so that she could recall what he looked like at will. She already knew he was average height with broad shoulders, and well-defined arm and thigh muscles. He had unruly, wavy brown hair and the most noticeable thing about him was that he was deeply tanned. She thought that this wasn't just holiday tanning, but that he probably worked outdoors. His features were regular but unremarkable, nothing outstandingly handsome or horrendous, but he had a bright smile and good, even teeth. Colour of eyes she wondered and was gazing thoughtfully at his head just as he turned round. Although embarrassed to be caught out, she managed to smile, unconcernedly.

'What's happening over there?'

'I think someone's had one too many, but nothing serious.'

She had the information; they were grey, but sparkling with light, not dull and dark.

'And you said you were thirsty, so do you...'

The rest of the sentence was drowned by Sam's voice cutting across the babble of conversation in the room.

'Simon, come on. Now please. Or you'll be walking.'

He looked startled, but shrugged and reached for his glass.

'Sorry, got to go.'

He gulped down the remains of his pint.

'Will you be here tomorrow? I think there's usually a good crowd on Saturdays.'

'Possibly, yes. But no promises. I may be too knackered after tonight!'

'Simon, move it.'

'Coming. Hope you do.'

And with a wave to the room in general, he was gone.

Gabriella sat quietly, sipping her drink. Well, well, she thought, you didn't expect to meet someone like that, did you? And why is a five-minute acquaintance such a big deal was the next question which raised its head. Yes, come on, what's this all about? Her analytical, work-brain was kicking in. He merely happens to be a pleasant young man whom you have met and who has asked you to have a drink. End of story. But she knew that her emotional-brain was telling her that the story could go on and that in this instance, it might be very pleasant if it did. She tried to stop the phrase "Mr Right" dancing round her brain.

Picking up her almost empty glass, she located a group of players who had come off court and weaved a path through the drinkers to join them. She was suddenly conscious of being on her own, making her way to a group of couples. Well, perhaps... Stop that, she inwardly remonstrated while putting on a smile and approaching George, Alice and a very pleasant couple whom she believed were called Mike and Su, but names and faces were beginning to blur a bit.

Conversation in the group was lively and she and Alice were just catching up on news of a mutual acquaintance when George butted in.

'By the way Gabriella, do you know who else belongs to the club?'

He didn't wait for any reply.

'Jason.'

'Jason? What Jason Bruce?'

'Yes,' it was Alice speaking now, 'your old partner.'

'Mind you,' George took a step closer and lowered his voice, 'he doesn't play, just comes in the bar as a social member and...' Gabriella looked mystified as George glanced around to make sure no one could overhear, 'he rather likes to...' he paused and lifted his right hand to his lips in the internationally recognised mime for drinking.

'Oh, I see.'

This was surprising news not least because Jason had been a good athlete in his teens, playing tennis at the club and rugby for Cadmore.

'He drinks too much.'

George positively winced at his wife's succinct appraisal of the situation.

'Er, just has a bit of difficulty knowing when to stop,' he finished lamely.

'Well, I know when to stop,' Gabriella laughed, putting her empty glass down on the table, 'so I'll say thanks for a very pleasant evening, I'm off home now.'

'When shall we see you again?'

'Oh, pretty soon. Definitely. My tennis needs all the help it can get. I'll, erm, probably be down tomorrow night.'

She turned and headed for the door, passing Tom Scotford on his way in looking somewhat angrily at his mobile phone.

'Are you leaving?'

'Yes.'

She could be equally brusque.

'Goodnight Gabriella Devonshire.'

He gave her an odd little smile and she didn't know if he was teasing her, possibly indicating that he had got her name exactly right. Ignoring him, she walked through the lobby and out, breathing in the still warm air of a beautiful evening. They were having a prolonged spell of dry, early summer weather and, as she walked to her car, Gabriella felt that life was suddenly pretty damn good.

She drove home, made some tea and took it up to her bedroom. Her body felt tired and a few aches were already creeping into muscles she hadn't used for a while. But her mind was buzzing, replaying what had happened, who she had met and what they had said. But all the time, she came back to Simon and, sipping her tea, had a delicious moment closing her eyes and mentally conjuring up his face again. Did she have a clear memory? Not quite. So all the more reason to pay more attention tomorrow! What a good thought.

She opened her eyes and smiled.

'You've gone a bit little-girly,' she admonished herself, 'why's that?'

It was a fair question, so she gave it some thought. He had been friendly and light-hearted, also he had been another single person about her age and an unexpected bonus so to speak. She conjectured whether Simon would be amused to think of himself as an unexpected bonus. But she knew she had been attracted to him, enjoyed his carefree attitude and when they had stood together in the middle of the court, also knew there was that indefinable "something" about the moment. For once, she seemed to have found someone who ticked all the right boxes. And now she was wondering how tomorrow would go because, even if she felt half crippled, she was definitely going back.

Tom drove home in a less than good mood, but that was often par for the course these days. He wasn't quite sure why he felt like this; perhaps he was extra tired after a fairly long and stressful week. No, he knew that wasn't it. He had a decision to make and it was crunch time. He did regret being quite so irritable with Caroline when she had rung just as he was going up to the clubhouse, but he really hadn't had the patience to listen to her banging-on about her wants and needs. And he had nearly bumped into that new girl who had just been leaving. He smiled as he remembered how she had advised him, in no uncertain terms, what she wanted to be called and he felt another twitch of amusement recalling the thunderous look she had given him when he had told her how to hit a forehand properly. And as well as her forehand, he had noticed her legs; he had not seen such lovely limbs in ages and the rest was pretty damn good too.

Game, Set and Love Match

CHAPTER 3

When the alarm shrilled in her right ear, Gabriella moaned, fumbled for the snooze switch and was preparing to turn over when she suddenly realised that it was Saturday. She stumbled out of bed, crossed the room and threw open the curtains. It was important to know what the weather was like – that the good spell hadn't come to end.

'Yes,' she exclaimed exultantly, 'yes, yes ,yes.'

It was sunny and dry, perfect weather.

Twenty minutes later she was in the kitchen, humming a little song and writing a shopping list while putting away two slices of toast and a mug of tea. To fill the day, it looked as though she ought to drive to the big shopping mall about ten miles away and have a good look round and lunch out. Still humming softly between gulps of cooling tea, she finished her list.

As she drove home through the mid-afternoon traffic, Gabriella was in a very good mood; the shopping had turned out to be quite successful and a new, rather smart linen dress was sitting in its carrier-bag on the back seat. Lunch had been in a small bistro where the waiter had been more attentive than need be, but it had all been a bit of a laugh, and now, showered and hair washed, she was preparing to have a quick sandwich before going out.

Glancing at the clock as she poured her tea, she wondered, not for the first time that day, what Simon was doing, what he liked doing in fact and where he lived and where he worked. There were so many things she had to find out about him and she also wondered whether he had thought about her. She desperately hoped there would be some way to get more chance to talk. Stuffing a piece of ham sandwich into her mouth, she chewed and swallowed quickly. That was the downside of meeting at the club, they were there to play tennis and that took up most of the time. The sandwich had gone and she finished the remains of her tea.

She glanced at the clock again. It was five-fifteen. Right, she felt herself going into action mode. Clattering her dirty dishes into the sink, she left them and larruped upstairs. Throwing off her bath robe, she pulled on her tennis clothes and wondered what to do with her hair tonight. Last night she had kept back her shoulder length blonde hair with a narrow band, so to be different, she secured it at the nape of her neck with a large tortoiseshell clip.

'Being a bit vain,' she admonished herself in the mirror, but it was now five-thirty and there was no time to bother with it any more. She ran downstairs, waved to Mrs Kennings, her neighbour, jumped in and slammed the car into gear.

Turning in through the club gates, she realised there was a bit of a knot in her stomach and her heart was pounding with anticipation.

'Oh no!'

The car park was entirely empty, she was far too early. Sitting, deflated, heart still pumping and feeling a bit of a fool, she surveyed the quiet scene. But then, to her surprise, another car drove in, parked up by the hedge and a man got out. She watched as he walked to the pavilion, unlocked it and walked back, disappearing behind the hedge in the direction of the clubhouse. Hallelujah for the caretaker or barman or whoever he was. Collecting her bag from the boot she made her way over to the silent building, remembering those previous years when she had walked through its doors on just such a fine evening.

Looking round and finding the supply of balls, she selected the best of a not very new-looking lot and walked out onto the farthest court. If she had been stupid enough to get here too early, then the least she could do was see how well her serve was going. The answer was soon very apparent, not as well as she would like and she was so totally engrossed that she didn't hear the rear gate click.

'You've got that action wrong.'

She jumped in fright at the sound of a voice, swivelling round to find Tom Scotford walking towards her.

'You're collapsing on the stroke and it's not good enough. Come here and I'll show you how it should be done.'

She looked at him, breathing heavily from exertion and now with suppressed rage.

'Come on,' she thought he had sensed that she was not overly pleased, 'you want to improve, don't you?'

'Yes,' she walked in his direction, 'alright, show me.'

She gave him a curt nod, expecting him to start serving himself. Instead he came towards her.

'Put your racket down.'

'What?'

He reached out and taking her racket, placed it on the ground with his.

'Now, like this.'

He suddenly moved behind her and, gripping her wrists in his hands, swung them with his into the arcing movements of the service stroke. She was being forced to reach so far upwards she thought her feet might leave the ground. The stretch and the difference in technique were amazing, dizzying even, and the strength of his body so close to hers was an incredible feeling. He released her hands and stepped back.

'Well, can you feel the difference?'

Wow, yes she certainly could feel things. Momentarily overcome she took a deep breath before collecting herself.

'Yes, yes I can. But I don't know if I can do it like that.'

He stared back at her.

'Why ever not? Of course you can, you just need to practice.'

And for the next ten minutes, he made her serve balls back to him. At first there was no improvement but, quite silently, he kept throwing balls to her to serve, time and time again. To begin with her anger at his unwelcome interference and criticism was still bubbling just below the surface, but she had been hooked by his comment about wanting to improve. She used to be a good player, and he didn't know that, so yes she did want to get back to her former standard. Gradually she adjusted to the new technique until she actually began to groove the serving action. Her anger had evaporated and she was concentrating on getting it right, every time, when he broke his silence.

'Better. Now, I think others are arriving, so we need to finish.'

They collected the balls and started to walk towards the pavilion. Did she have to be polite? Probably.

'Well, thanks for the lesson. I'll try to put it into practice tonight.'

'Good.'

It was all the reply she got and again she felt mildly irritated by this rather taciturn man.

However, she didn't have time to waste on him as she was waiting for Simon's appearance and hoped he wouldn't be long. But others started to arrive and she soon found herself playing doubles with George, Alice and Mike where it was much more difficult both to keep watch on the entrance and try to serve properly when she remembered. Time was passing and he still didn't arrive and little fingers of despair were starting to clutch at her heart. She was playing again, keeping an ear tuned for Sam's pretty distinctive and loud voice, but there was no welcome sound of a strident laugh or a shouted remark. Sighing in frustration, she tossed a ball high into the air, reached up and banged a positive sidewinder of a serve past George on the other side of the net. It only made her feel a bit better.

Eventually, she and Mike managed to beat George and Alice and they straggled off court and headed for the benches. Still no sign.

'You were serving well tonight.'

Mike had dropped onto a seat beside his wife, who had been sitting out, and Gabriella had joined them.

'Yes, it must be the Scotford magic paying off.'

'The what?'

Two pairs of eyes were directed towards her. She then had to explain about her over-early arrival and the coaching session.

'You were here alone with Tom Scotford? '

Su's eyes were wide.

'How did you manage to concentrate on tennis?'

Gabriella was mystified.

'Quite easily, why would it be difficult?'

Mike started to chuckle.

'Gabriella, don't tell me you're the only woman here who doesn't think Tom is drop dead gorgeous.'

He shot an amused look at his wife – the words were obviously a quote.

'Well, he's alright I suppose.'

Su looked at her incredulously.

'Gabriella, he's fabulous, we're all madly in love with him.'

Gabriella, amazed, looked questioningly at Mike. He grinned back at her and shrugged.

'It's true. He's like a Greek god to them, even Alice. Get her going about him when George isn't around. You'll be surprised.'

He laughed again obviously amused by her surprise.

'Oh, come on. Don't you really think he's good-looking, athletic, charming?'

'Possibly he is, I mean, yes he's certainly good-looking, those blue eyes are quite stunning, but he seemed a bit aloof, even taciturn with me. Have to admit he's a good player though. But,' she paused as though making sure what she was saying was what she felt, 'I can honestly say I haven't been in line for any of the charm.'

She turned grinning towards Su.

'Perhaps he's used it all up on the rest of you.'

'Oh Gabriella. He makes me go weak at the knees.'

'Really? Well, I have to tell you that my knees remained quite unbuckled.'

There were snorts of laughter and Mike was about to say something else when she saw Simon walking in through the gate, swinging a racket, and on his own.

'Oh, Simon's come at last.'

It was an involuntary remark, a release of anxiety and she felt her face colour. Mike looked at her and she knew she had betrayed her happiness. It was almost an acknowledgement to herself that she had been waiting for "Mr Right" to turn up – literally.

'Su.'

His wife looked up at her husband who was rising from his seat.

'Come into the pavilion and take a look at a bit of a sore spot I can feel on my toe. See if it needs anything doing to it.'

Gabriella looked up at him. She was sure it was a lie, but she was so grateful to him if it was.

'Hi. I'm sorry to be so late.'

Simon eased onto the empty seat beside her.

'Got a phone call just as I was getting ready and then I realised the socks I was putting on were odd ones and had to hunt for a pair. Pathetic isn't it? Sorry, again, though.'

He was smiling and his grey eyes were sparkling and she couldn't have cared less whether he had odd socks on or not.

'And you're on your own tonight?'

'Yep. Sam and Brian have had to wait in for a visitor or something; they'll be down a bit later on.'

'Now you two,' George was leaning out of the pavilion doorway, 'would you like to mix in please?'

Gabriella didn't particularly care whether she played or not, but thought she ought to show willing.

Towards the end of the evening, Gabriella and Simon had both managed to convince George that they didn't really need to play any more.

'Shall we go for a drink now? You don't particularly want to watch do you?'

Her heart did that little lurching thing and she wondered if she was blushing a bit. But, whatever she might be looking like, Gabriella had no intention of watching other people when she could be having a drink with Simon. They walked together up the path, fronds of the huge Leylandii hedge brushing their faces, chatting inconsequentially.

When they got inside, she insisted on getting the drinks and again they found themselves sitting in a quiet corner and, as they continued to chat and relax together, Gabriella could imagine the rest of the summer months stretching away in similar, idyllic fashion. He was so easy to talk to and they laughed and shared jokes together as though they had been friends for years. She thought he was looking at her with something that was a bit more than just a friendly expression and she suddenly held her breath when he reached towards her face with his hand.

'You've got a stray twig caught in your hair.'

And as he brushed it out, her mind went into overdrive imagining that hand continuing to stroke her cheek and … she stopped the fantasy right there.

It was getting difficult to concentrate as the noise in the room was increasing, but that was fine because it meant they had to lean closer to hear. She found out that he liked walking and had done a bit of mountaineering but didn't really have time for it any more and said he wasn't fit enough anyway. Suddenly she remembered where they had left off their last conversation.

'I've told you what I do, so tell me about your job. I'm going to stick my neck out and say I don't think it's in an office.'

He laughed and told her that she was one hundred per cent right.

'I'm an engineer on an oil rig in the North Sea.'

The words hit her like a North Sea blast and an icy frost seemed to be encircling her heart. Stunned, she could hardly believe what he had said. Trying not to show her absolute dismay, her eyes widened with amazement and alarm.

'The North Sea?

She tried to collect her spinning thoughts.

'Then what are you doing in Upton Peploe?'

There seemed to be no noise now in the room, just the thumping of her heart. She listened with an increasing sense of despair and loss as Simon explained that he was on a short holiday from his job in the North Sea and had come to Upton Peploe to help his sister Sam and brother-in-law move house. He'd been playing as their guest and was leaving tomorrow.

'I can't imagine working in such a hostile environment,' she said with a little shiver, trying to find something sensible to say that would disguise her unhappiness at this unexpected news. There was a dark hole appearing in her life, where previously things had seemed to be going so well for once. He laughed, seeming not to have noticed her distress.

'But you want your home to be lit and heated, don't you?'

'I do.'

Her brain managed to think of something quick-witted and humorous.

'And I shall think of you each time I boil an egg!'

She forced herself to smile, get the room, which had seemed to disappear, back into focus, and was aware that if he had stayed, she could have enjoyed her time with easy-going Simon. And she wondered whether they would have done more than just play tennis together and realised that she had already been there in her imagination.

They both drank silently for a moment and then, as though acknowledging some sort of unspoken agreement, made a determined effort to keep the conversation light and meaningless. She could sense that he was looking at her, perhaps wondering whether they ought to pick up the threads of anything more personal again or whether the moment had really gone.

'Time to go, brother.'

Sam was standing by the clubhouse door with Brian, who was waving his car keys in the air in an exaggerated manner. Yes, the moment had gone.

'Well,' she said, thinking fast to cover what she was really feeling, 'this means we won't be able to have that re-match after all.'

He stood and smiled down at her.

'Afraid not, but I did really enjoy my time here. Thanks a lot Gabriella.'

And he leant over and kissed her on the cheek before waving his goodbyes to the room. There was a blistering heat of fire where he had touched her with his lips and a dark chasm of emptiness inside her as she watched him disappear through the doorway, out into the night and back to the North Sea.

'Please stay safe,' she murmured.

She sat for a while trying to regain her composure and put right out of her mind the future which had started to form with Simon as a part of it. After several minutes, quickly draining the last drops of juice from her glass, she thumped it down on the table and walked towards the door.

'Are you off?' Mike was watching her leave.

'Yes, goodbye all, see you next week I expect,' and she opened the inner door and stepped through into the lobby She felt devastated.

Standing for a moment, zipping up her tracksuit top before making her exit, she heard the door of the Gents bang and saw a just recognisable figure, as a portly Jason lurched unsteadily into the lobby. Surprisingly, he recognised her immediately.

'Ah ha, Gab-rella. Hey. What a nice bit of stuff you've turned into. H'lo Come 'n' haf a drink.'

He was shouting and waving his arms, more for balance than in greeting she thought.

'No thanks, Jason. I' m just going.'

She started to sidestep round the swaying figure when he stumbled, reached out and grabbed her. But then he held on, looking at her with leering, barely focussing eyes.

'Gi's a kiss.'

His beery breath hit her in the face, it was revolting; but worse was the feeling of his hand now rasping up her thigh and starting to fumble with her skirt.

'Stop it, get away. Let go!'

She was already raw from Simon's departure and the drunken attentions of Jason were the last straw. Furious rather than afraid, she twisted away from his grasp, lashed out with a free hand and caught him a thumping blow across a roughly-stubbled cheek.

'You're drunk, you fool. Get away from me, Jason.'

She was about to make for the outer door again when, suddenly, Jason was in an armlock and being propelled forcefully towards the exit. The look on his face as this tall, blonde stranger effortlessly manhandled him outside would have been laughable in different circumstances.

'Get out and don't you dare touch that young lady again. Do you understand?'

Tom's voice was low but so cold and steely it almost made Gabriella feel frightened.

'Bit o' fun, thash all,' she heard Jason shouting as the door closed behind him.

Mike had now also appeared from the bar and the two men looked at her in concern.

'Are you O.K? What happened?'

Mike was looking anxiously at her.

'Yes, yes, I'm fine. Just had a bit of an argument with Jason. Tom sent him packing.' She looked at him.

'Thanks for intervening.'

'No problem. I didn't realise you had quite such a good left hook. I must remember not to annoy you, Gabriella.'

Although now feeling a bit shocked by the encounter, she managed to smile.

'I hope it hurt him a bit anyway.'

Tom glanced at Mike who was still looking anxiously on.

'I'm just leaving, so I'll walk out to the car park and make sure our resident inebriate has departed.'

Mike nodded and looked relieved.

'Right. OK, if all's well, I'll get back. Goodnight both.'

Tom held the door open.

'Do you need a lift?'

'No, no, I've got a car in the car park, thanks.'

They walked out into cooler air. There was no sign of Jason.

'Were you going home with him?'

'What? No. He came out of the cloakroom as I was leaving and wanted me to have a drink.'

'I see. So where's your boyfriend, why isn't he looking after you?'

She stopped walking and looked uncomprehendingly at him.

'I don't know what you mean?'

'The young man, Simon.'

She drew in a breath.

'Not boyfriend and he's gone. Gone back to the North Sea.'

'He's done what?'

She realised how odd that must have sounded, took another deep breath and launched into an explanation.

'He's an engineer. He works on an oil rig in the North Sea.'

Then just to make things absolutely clear.

'He's been here helping his sister to move house.'

'Oh.'

They walked past the pavilion in silence and Gabriella found her car keys in a pocket and pressed the fob, seeing the little lights of her small, yellow convertible wink in welcome.

'Is that yours?'

'Yes.'

She saw a slow smile spread across his face.

'What a spunky little car. Just right for you Gabriella.'

She was a bit amazed. That almost seemed like a compliment from him. He stepped up to the driver's door and held it open for her.

'I should have checked that you're OK to drive. Are you?'

She was already sinking into the driver's seat.

'Yes, perfectly thanks.'

She had switched on the ignition emphasising that she was ready to go.

'Goodnight and ... thanks again.'

'My pleasure.'

He shut the door and she accelerated out from the car park and through the gates. Her response hadn't been entirely truthful as she was beginning to feel a bit shaky but, determined to concentrate for five minutes or so and not recall the evening's dismal events yet, she headed for home. Men! Why did people think she needed one in her life? The trouble was - she had almost started to believe she did.

Tom watched the rear lights disappear before walking to his car, starting up and making his own way home. He was deep in thought. Arriving home and opening the front door, he walked straight into his study, switched on the computer and waited. He had been too indecisive of late, things needed sorting and that was what he must do. Looking at his diary for the coming week, he could see an opportunity. He was going to Amsterdam for a one-day visit on Thursday, so, if he stayed up in London, he could book a restaurant table for Friday and then come home on Saturday morning. Yes, that would all work. He went to bed, thinking about the possibility of doing a bit of light gardening tomorrow as things were starting to look parched and bedraggled and he was also clear about what he needed to achieve next week.

By early Monday morning Tom was at his desk, ready to start both the firm's work and the sort-your-life-out tasks he had set himself.

If asked, most people would say, unequivocally, that Tom Scotford had a pretty good life and he had to acknowledge that he was extremely fortunate. Good job with a salary and bonuses to go with it, nice house and any car which took his fancy when he wanted to renew the current model. But his life recently had not been going as it should – drifting, in fact. He knew why and he knew the solution; get on and take the action which he had been putting off for at least the last two months and which he had decided must now be tackled head-on. He glanced at his watch, Caroline would be at work and he reached for his mobile.

'Tom, sorry to disturb you.'

The Managing Director's PA had put her head round the door.

'Come in Fredi, you can't disturb someone who's not quite got started yet, what can I do for you?'

Frederika Malsoe stepped into his office and not for the first time Tom wondered how this mother of four managed to look so well turned out, unruffled and cheerful as well as running things with total efficiency.

'Nothing too much,' she smiled, 'Max has just found these tickets for the theatre which he had forgotten about and hopes you can make use of them. With his compliments. But it's a bit short notice as they're for this Saturday.'

Ah, he thought, Saturday's not too good. Pity.

'Why can't Max use them?'

'He forgot to tell his wife about them and she's accepted an invitation to a house party in Suffolk for the weekend '

'Oh dear.'

He glanced at the tickets which she had placed on his desk.

'Bloody hell, this show's virtually sold out and has had rave reviews.'

'I know. Can't you use them, Tom?'

He thought for a moment.

'Yes, leave them with me. I think I can do something with them.'

'Good. Thanks.'

She was about to leave but turned at the door.

'Tom. Are you OK?'

He looked up, startled.

'Yes, Fredi. Why do you ask?'

She shrugged.

'It's just that you've seemed a bit low, a bit out of sorts lately. Just wondered if you were OK that's all.'

He smiled at her.

'Thanks. Yes, I'm OK just sorting out one or two things. Which reminds me, I want to change my leave dates from the two weeks in August to sometime later, probably September or October. Can you let me know if that'll be a problem?'

'Will do. Can't think it'll be any trouble.'

The door closed and Tom sat, nonplussed. If people were noticing a change in him then he hadn't been disguising his feelings as well as he'd imagined. He looked at the tickets, picked them up and placed them into his briefcase. Then he reached for his mobile, hesitated and stopped.

'Tom Scotford, do some work,' he said to the empty office.

Wednesday, halfway through the week. He stretched, looked at his watch and started to pack up, realising that if he was very quick, he could be on the five-forty-five train home. Just making it onto the platform with a couple of minutes to spare, he jostled onto the train along with all the other eponymous commuters: ladies who had come up to London for some shopping, tourists returning from seeing the sights and students who seemed always to be 'plugged in' and largely oblivious to their surroundings. Finding a seat, he sank into it. The advantage of the five-forty-five was that it was a fast train and that would mean he could be at the club by seven or thereabouts. He wondered how Gabriella had been. In fact he had been wondering that for the last three and a half days. Thinking back to Saturday night, he could still see the forlorn look on her face when she'd said, "He's gone back to the North Sea." What with that and then Jason leaping, well figuratively speaking, out at her, she must be feeling pretty down. If she was at the club, he could check she was alright. Then, remembering the startled look on Jason's face when she swung a left at him, he started to smile. If there was a young woman who had the capacity to bounce back from adversity, he reckoned she might be Gabriella, never call me Gaby, Devonshire.

He was later than he had expected when he drove through the gates and found a space. The parking area was nearly full, but a quick, visual check told him that there was no yellow convertible among the cars yet. He had a bit of a bad feeling about this. Perhaps he'd been wrong. He didn't have time for further conjecture as George was hurrying from the pavilion towards his car looking pretty harassed. As he got out from the driver's seat, he had a distinctly uneasy feeling that something was wrong.

'Ah, Tom. So glad you're here. We've had a spot of bother I need to tell you about.'

'What sort of bother, George?'

'Well, it's Jason.'

Tom froze, he couldn't believe that Jason had gone after Gabriella again.

'What's he done?'

His voice was low and full of suppressed anger.

'He's attacked…'

'Who?'

Tom was almost shouting now.

'Who's that drunken oaf attacked?'

George stepped back a little, hit by the ferocity of the words and was looking apprehensively at Tom.

'He's punched the barman because he refused to serve him any more. He's broken the poor man's nose.'

'Oh.'

Tom had to stop himself saying "good," because it wasn't Gabriella. He looked at George who still seemed terribly distressed as though Jason's actions had caused him personal, physical harm. He collected his thoughts and spoke in a more reasonable manner.

'So what's going to happen now?'

George sighed heavily and a bit theatrically.

'Oh, I've already revoked his membership, and if anyone sees him down here, I or Mike or someone must be alerted immediately. I can't have this sort of thing happening and I gather from Mike he attacked Gabriella last week and you got rid of him then.'

Tom nodded, suddenly realising what Jason might have done to Gabriella if he had been drunk enough or angry enough.

'I should have been told,' George was adding huffily, 'Gabriella should have made a complaint.'

'I don't think she thought it was too serious and luckily, it wasn't on that occasion.' He suddenly saw an opportunity.

'Does she know about this? Has she been down since?'

'No, I've left a message on her home phone and rather hoped she would be here tonight. She hasn't turned up yet, but perhaps she'll be down later on.'

Tom doubted that. Gabriella had seemed to get to the club reasonably early and he didn't expect her to arrive now that it was nearly quarter to eight. They were nearing the pavilion. He needed to act, wanted some information and thought he could just see a way.

'George, I need to speak to Gabriella about a work-related matter. If I can have her phone number, I'll just check that she's alright if you like.'

George seemed terribly grateful that someone was sharing the burden he obviously felt and brightened.

'Oh that would be really good if you wouldn't mind. I've got the number in the Members' Book, come inside and I'll find it now.'

During the evening, the conversation naturally turned to the Jason incident and news soon got round about what had happened with Gabriella. Mike and Tom found themselves re-telling the incident and Tom noted that there was a genuine concern for Gabriella and some anxiety that she hadn't been seen since. He heard people voicing the opinion that "someone" ought to do "something." He, however, did not feel it necessary to tell them that he intended to do just that.

Play finished a bit earlier than usual and few people seemed to want to hang around. Making his goodbyes and muttering something about having some work-calls to make, he excused himself from the small group who were going up to the clubhouse and sauntered back to his car. He got home just before nine, made coffee and settled into his favourite leather recliner. Taking out the scrap of paper George had given him, which was a landline and not the mobile number he had hoped for, he punched in the numbers. He heard incessant ringing and was expecting an answerphone to click in.

'Hello.'

Gabriella sounded quite breathless, but at least she was there.

'Gabriella, hello. Hope I haven't disturbed you too much. It's Tom.'

He heard another catch of breath.

'No, not at all, I was just coming in and heard the phone ringing as I had my key in the lock, so a bit of a scramble, that's all. How are you?'

'That's the question I'm supposed to be asking you,' he laughed. 'I've been to the club, heard the news from George and people are a bit worried that they haven't seen you and hope you're feeling alright.'

'Oh, that's so very nice of folks.'

She sounded genuinely touched.

'Yes, I'm fine. A bit tired as I've been doing overtime at work for the last two evenings, helping my boss get a big piece of work finished. So nothing wrong. Thanks.'

'Good. That's good. Now, if you've just got in, I won't keep you too long, but I wondered if you could do me a sort of favour.'

He had thought long and hard how he was going to broach this and had decided on that particular tack.

'A favour? Well...well yes, if I can.'

Having secured that agreement in principle, he told her he had two theatre tickets and explained that he had wondered whether she would like a pleasant Saturday night experience this week to counteract the rather unpleasant one from last week. Then he played what he hoped might be a trump card and told her what the show was.

'Oh my word, that show's supposed to be one of the best things ever. I thought it was sold out for months ahead. Have you really got tickets?'

He could sense her excitement. Telling her how he had come by them, he asked the big question.

'So are you free to come with me, please?'

Gabriella had by now got over the initial surprise, and was starting to think this through. Basically it was a fantastic offer and in some ways, although she had never rated Tom as one of her most favourite people, he had helped with the Jason fracas and if he needed a favour, then it would be a way of repaying him. Besides, the show was getting outstanding reviews and it didn't really matter who was taking you to see it.

'Tom, thank you for thinking of me. Yes, please, I would really like to go.'

He gave her details of timings and finally asked if she would be going to the club before the weekend.

'I do think people would like to see you again. I have commitments on Friday and won't make it.'

'I'll see. Depends how work goes. I know we'll go on late tomorrow but Friday might be OK.'

'Good. Well I'll let you get in properly now. And thanks again. I'll look forward to Saturday. Goodnight Gabriella.'

She wished him goodnight, put the phone down and turned back to lock the front door which was still swinging open.

'Life's full of surprises at the moment,' she muttered, 'some nice, some not so. And some quite unexpected! Don't quite know what to make of it.'

Walking with her bags into the kitchen, she put the kettle on, unpacked the shopping and laid up a supper tray.

CHAPTER 4

On Thursday morning, she was in the office and had been working on stuff for Steve for nearly an hour before he stuck his head round her door.

'How're you fixed for overtime still?'

'Not a problem. Was expecting to work late tonight and then thought you'd tell me what you need me to do on Friday.'

Steve lowered himself into a chair opposite and thought for a moment.

'I think we shall be nearly done by Friday and I'd rather you had some time to catch up on the stuff we've let slip a bit, so you can decide whether you need to work late or not. Is that OK? I know you'll be missing your tennis. How's it going by the way? Shall I see you at Wimbledon in the near future?'

'Only eating over-priced strawberries with the rest of the hoi polloi,' she laughed.

'But, since you ask, my tennis has improved a bit, which is just as well, because it had provoked serious criticism from the club's best player.'

Having said that, she had to recount her initial meeting with Tom Scotford and his subsequent coaching. She didn't say any more because, even though Gabriella considered Steve as a good friend as well as her boss, she decided that the bit about the surprising theatre invitation was private, nothing that anyone else need know. So once Steve had left, she re-applied herself to employment law and its ramifications.

Although she could have gone to the club on Friday, she decided against it. She knew why. Talk would inevitably drift to what folks were doing at the weekend and she somehow didn't want to tell them that she was being taken to the theatre by Tom Scotford. For one thing, they would rib her mercilessly and read all sorts of wrong things into a very simple social arrangement. She remembered that Tom was not going to be around, so all should pass off without causing comment, which was how she thought everyone should be able to go about their business.

Back in his office early-ish on Friday, Tom worked on notes from his meetings in Amsterdam, sorting out the questions which had been raised during his visit and making some preliminary recommendations. At just after nine, Fredi put her head round his door.

'How was Amsterdam?'

'Wet,' he grinned, 'but all seems to be going well over there, which is good news.'

'Max will see you for a debrief at noon or five-thirty.'

He chose noon, and was about to continue with his notes when he realised he hadn't checked his phone messages last night and there might be some alteration to his evening plans. There were several messages including the one he was really looking for confirming that his own text had been received and agreeing the restaurant at eight. He sat back in his chair. Several scenarios crossed his mind, but, clear about what he wanted to achieve, he decided not to form any master-plan but just to wait and play it by ear.

By six, he joined the melee of commuters jam-packed on the tube, got off a stop early and walked back to his hotel. He had time for a short rest before he needed to change but decided to re-set the alarm in case he fell heavily asleep. When the metallic ringing did wake him, he rolled off the bed, into the bathroom, stepped into the shower and forced himself to have it colder than he wanted. Taking a clean shirt off the hanger, he rummaged for a different tie and retrieved his trousers from the press. The suit was beginning to look a bit lived in, but it would have to do for tonight. He wondered if that would be noticed. Expect so, he thought. Ah well, home tomorrow, very quick turnaround and then the theatre trip. He suddenly realised he had set himself quite a schedule, but it would be worth it. Oh yes, it would all be worth it.

On Saturday her doorbell rang at four-thirty and Gabriella opened it to see a taxi waiting outside and Tom on the doorstep. She locked up and he walked beside her down the path.

'Gabriella, you look very nice.'

Great, she thought, a real compliment at last and the new linen dress had obviously been the right choice. He was smiling at her and she looked at him: beautiful pale shirt, lightweight suit and a colourful patterned silk tie.

'You too, Mr Scotford. I think this is the first time I've seen you wearing clothes. NO, that's not what I mean!'

But he was laughing uproariously as he helped her into the taxi. She, however, felt a wave of pure embarrassment flow over her at the picture she had conjured up.

'I'm sorry, you know I meant rather than tennis kit.'

But he was still laughing and, having got them off to that start, they continued to burst into little fits of giggles while Jon, their driver, took them to the station.

There were not many travellers waiting for the London train at this time of day and she had an unpleasant flashback remembering Mark Haddon. But this was different today. She had already noted that they were standing on the platform where the First Class carriages would pull in. Mmm, she thought to herself, these are the little luxuries that money can buy and made a mental note to find out exactly what Tom did. Whatever it was, it seemed to buy excellent clothes, expensive tennis rackets and...she realised that she had no idea what sort of car, except that it was silver.

'Here it comes.'

The train was arriving and shortly Tom was leading her towards a carriage, finding seats and making sure she was settled comfortably. One of the things which Gabriella had noticed about him, besides the intense colour of the eyes, was that he was extremely courteous, and she rather liked that.

Once in London she was immediately hit, again, by the humidity, hustle and noise. Whenever she came into the city, there always seemed to be so many people all snaking in different directions and generally barring the route she wanted to take. But Tom guided her out of the station, through the eddying knots of sightseeing tourists and hailed them another taxi. Unlike Jon, this driver seemed intent on slewing around corners, darting up narrow side streets, cutting into queues of near-stationary vehicles and driving so close to the car in front that they almost looked like one articulated vehicle. Mercifully he decanted them in one piece in a quiet street where Gabriella gazed at the black and gold canopy over the door of "La Lune" restaurant.

'This looks rather nice.'

'I hope you think so. It's quite small, but they do good food here, French...will that be alright?'

'Almost any sort of food's alright with me,' she volunteered as they entered what was a more spacious interior than she had imagined, light and airy with ceiling fans thrumming gently and a black-aproned waiter moving towards them. Settled at a table, she glanced appreciatively around.

'The French just seem to do understated elegance so much better than we do, this is really lovely. Do you come here often as they say?'

Tom explained that he had used the restaurant quite frequently when he lived in London and had always liked it. Gabriella looked up from the menu she was studying.

'I don't know how you can live and work in a big city. I think it would drive me crazy.'

He laughed.

'Well I only work here now and I suppose the reason I moved out to Upton Peploe to live was to get a better balance in life.'

He didn't elaborate on the more complex reasons for moving and the wine waiter was hovering. They chose to drink Kir as an aperitif and spent a quiet few minutes selecting starters and mains.

'Now you know what you're eating, would you have any preference for wine?'

'Yes. My preference would be for you to choose, please.'

'Right. I'll do my best.'

As they sipped their drinks, Tom asked her what she did and she found herself explaining the job of Human Resources Analyst again. He seemed to grasp its essentials and asked about the other people in the office and whether they ever encountered any HR problems of their own. Then, before Gabriella could fire in any similar questions, they started chatting about the club and what it had been like when Gabriella had played there as a junior.

'How have you found it, coming back? I mean people often say that's a bad or at least a difficult thing to do.'

It was an interesting question and Gabriella took a moment to consider whether she would answer it fully or not. Beginning by explaining that yes, she had been a bit thrown by the changes and by the fact that she felt like an outsider this time, she then decided to go for it. She looked directly at him.

'I found you a bit off-putting.'

'Goodness. Why?'

He looked genuinely shocked.

'You were a bit brusque when we first met. Not rude or anything, but not very friendly and welcoming. And critical of my forehand.'

She had intended that as a bit of a joke to let the matter pass, but he was staring at her, dismay etched on his face.

'Gabriella, I'm truly sorry. I had no idea I was coming across like that. I did want you to improve because I could see you were a good player, just a bit out of practice. I'm so sorry if I offended you.'

He looked quite abject.

'Don't worry,' she smiled at him, 'you were absolutely right about the tennis and you managed to kick-start my competitive streak, so I am actually grateful now. And,' she continued before he could say anything else, 'I did get a different slant on you from constantly being told how absolutely fabulous you were by all the other women. Quite a fan- club you've got.'

'A what?'

His eyes were wide in amazement and Gabriella suddenly realised that this man possibly didn't know the effect he was having on women.

'The other ladies at the club. They talk about you endlessly and it's very flattering stuff.'

She was enjoying herself enormously now.

'You should hear the things they say.'

'Well, as I obviously don't, you're just going to have to tell me, aren't you?'

He had recovered his composure but she could tell that he was intrigued.

'Well. They do refer to you as the Upton Peploe Greek god.'

'Oh dear.'

He was now looking embarrassed.

'And the men say they're tired of hearing about "drop dead gorgeous Tom."'

He was looking hard at the table but she could see his lips twitch with amusement.

'Oh, and Alice told me that you'd make a very good catch for someone.'

His head jerked up, eyes narrowed a little.

'And what did Miss Devonshire say to that?'

She put on her most insouciant expression.

'I told her she made you sound like a prize haddock.'

He started to laugh, tears rolled, he coughed and almost choked. The waiters stepped forward anxiously but he waved them away, taking out a handkerchief.

'Oh my, oh, oh dear,' he wheezed breathily, 'how to be brought down to earth.'

The waiters, seeing that their client seemed to have recovered and was not in mortal danger, arrived with their starters.

'It was a good joke sir?'

'Yes, a very good one. This is a very amusing lady. Now,' he looked at her, 'shall we eat?'

'This is so good.'

Gabriella had paused after a couple of mouthfuls of salmon roulade and some exquisite little salad things dotted round the plate.

'I hope yours is.'

Tom nodded, totally happy with her pleasure in the food and the surroundings and her ability to convey the good time she was having. He was about to make a comparison in his mind, but stuffed the thought away and concentrated on his terrine instead and the enjoyable and entertaining time he was having.

'Tell me,' Gabriella was placing her knife and fork down on an extremely clean plate, 'I know you work in London and I think someone said it's in a bank. Is it?'

'No, not really. I mean, it's a financial institution, let's see – the easy way of describing it is like a sort of consultancy for investors. We do the research and analysis for them, write reports and offer our recommendations.'

'You're making it sound easy; I bet it's pretty complicated.'

He laughed.

'Yes, and boring to the outsider I think.'

'Why do you say that?'

'Because I've seen so many eyes glaze over if I go into more detail and anyway, it's a Saturday, so not a time for talking about work.'

Despite his protestations, she persisted with a few more questions and found that he generally worked long hours, except on some Wednesdays or Fridays when he got back early to play tennis, was often away for meetings and conferences, had been there four years and, surprisingly to her, thoroughly enjoyed it all.

Sitting back in her chair, she picked up her glass.

'That was absolutely one of the best meals ever. That duck was gorgeous and I was very right to get you to choose the wine. Superb.'

He proffered the bottle but she shook her head.

'No, thanks. I might fall asleep in the theatre and that would be awful as I'm so looking forward to the show.'

Despite the waiter's entreaties, they passed on any more food, just ordering coffee. When it arrived, Tom motioned the waiter to leave it, and as he poured her coffee, Gabriella was surprised at how easily he did things. But then, she realised, this was a man who was used to moving, normally and effortlessly, in situations and places such as this.

At the end of the performance, the whole audience rose to its feet to applaud and salute the cast. Tom had often stolen quick glances at her during the play and noticed how she was totally absorbed by it, watching with rapt attention, living it all as the actors wove the web of humour and tragedy on the stage. Not for the first time that day he silently thanked Max for his forgetfulness. Once the applause had died away, the lights came up and there was the usual crush and scuffle of people getting to the exits. He took her arm to steady her in the crowd, despite knowing she was quite capable of making her way unaided and, he also knew, possibly giving anyone who was too pushy a bit of a hand-off as well! Once outside, plunged into the still-humid air, they milled, with the rest of the audience, round the corner and out into a wider pavement area.

'We can walk to the end of this road and get a taxi or it's about ten minutes to the station on foot. Your choice.'

'Happy to walk.'

He had relinquished her arm but occasionally put a guiding hand on her shoulder as they walked slowly past pavement cafes and bars thumping out indecipherable lyrics to harsh rhythmic beats. She looked up at him.

'Tom, thank you so much for this, for inviting me. It's been so fantastic. I couldn't imagine anything like that. When they were about to shoot the horse I thought I would stand up and yell, "Stop!" The whole thing was just so…so incredible, so inventive, so wonderful. Did you like it?'

He was surprised at how moved he was by her words of completely sincere praise. He suddenly realised how delightful it was to take someone out who enjoyed things and looked at them with an open, appreciative nature. He felt ashamed at how he took so much of his life for granted.

'Yes, yes I did. You're right. It was a special thing to see. It's been a very good day.' He really meant that; it had been an absolute pleasure to share it. He hadn't told her of the rush he'd had to get back from London in the morning, change and be ready to return for the theatre.

The last few days, he thought, as their train pulled out of the station, had been quite extraordinary - almost too much to fit in, but it had all worked. Yes, indeed it had.

'Have you got a busy week coming up?'

Gabriella's sleepy voice brought him back to the present.

'Not quite so hectic,' he smiled at the understatement, 'but a bit busy, so I don't think I'll get down to the club until Wednesday. So make sure the weather stays fine, please.'

* * *

Over the next few days Tom did a lot of thinking. On Sunday when he worked, alone, in his garden, he had sorted out his thoughts, formed a plan of action and was in that wonderful state of anticipation, ready to put things in motion and see what would happen.

On Monday morning, he had just got started on a report when there was a light tap on the door and Max walked in.

'Morning Tom, have you anything very pressing on this week?'

As ever, Max could skip the pleasantries if there were work issues to discuss.

'No, nothing pressing, except this report and I shall have that done by lunch-time tomorrow, I think. Why?'

He knew Max was not just checking whether he had enough on to keep him gainfully employed.

'Oh, it's the Edinburgh Roadshow on Thursday and Friday and I would like you to go, please.'

'But I thought Brendan was doing that one?'

Edinburgh was not in his newly-formed plans for the week and he couldn't understand why his boss was suddenly making this apparent change.

'Yes, yes, he is, but it's the first one he's done and,' Max was strolling round the office and suddenly turned with what Tom recognised as his rather satisfied expression on his face.

'I've got a couple of new clients on board for it and I want your expertise available as well. I'll come up for the Friday.'

'Ah, so we're pushing the boat out a bit?'

Max smiled, almost conspiratorially.

'Just doing good business, young man, just doing good business. Anyway, check details with Fredi and I'll see you on Friday.'

He walked to door and then paused.

'Do you drink single malt by the way?

'No, never developed a taste for it.'

'Ah, pity. Might have to educate you.'

And he disappeared.

Tom, staring at the closed door, banged his forehead with his fist. This was not in his plans. Not at all. He was about to go into a mini-sulk when he realised there was no good reason why he couldn't still accomplish the personal tasks he had set himself, (there was the letter to write and the phone call to make,) he relaxed, knowing he could still keep on track, despite Edinburgh.

On Wednesday lunch-time he was making his way to the airport, having the afternoon to travel, settle in to his hotel, touch base with Brendan and get through Thursday and Friday. He was over his initial annoyance about the trip and was feeling more exhilarated than he had for ages. The sense of drift in his life had gone and he was looking forward to a new direction, quite what it would bring was uncertain, but he felt he had woken up, "smelt the coffee" and was ready for this new phase and new adventure.

By the same Wednesday lunch-time Gabriella was wondering where this week was speeding off to. But, sitting in front of her computer, she forked a bit of salad into her mouth, hoping to get on and be away by five if she could. She nearly accomplished that, getting home just before six.

When she arrived at the club later than expected, she was surprised that there weren't many people actually playing. Walking into the pavilion, she was greeted by Su and Alice, who said they were pleased to see her after "recent events" and then immediately offered the news that Tom wasn't here and they were all wondering where he was. Although really nothing to do with her, Gabriella felt slightly cross on his behalf. She firmly believed that everyone had a right to a reasonably private life and she didn't see that Tom should have to account for his movements all the time.

'Perhaps he's just enjoying a bit of pleasant time on his own, not at everyone's beck and call.'

She hadn't meant to say that and could see the rather startled expressions on the other women's faces.

'Anyway, why don't we go and knock a few balls about,' she hastily added, not wanting this to become any sort of issue. Alice gave her a bit of an old-fashioned look, but the three of them walked out together and all seemed relaxed and friendly enough.

Tom's absence though turned into the main topic of conversation and although she knew he had intended to come down that evening, Gabriella was quite aware that things can change and there could be heaps of reasons why he hadn't turned up. She tried hard not to make any more caustic comments as she could see Alice and Su look warily at her whenever someone voiced the question, 'Does anyone know what's happened to Tom tonight?'

The tennis was alright and because there were fewer people down, she played all evening and then joined the group going up to the clubhouse for a drink.

'Su tells me you told her and Alice off.'

Mike was standing beside her at the bar as they were collecting drinks on a tray.

'Yes, she grinned, 'I don't think they realised that the right to personal privacy pushes all my buttons.'

Mike nodded.

'You're right, we do tend to make Tom public property and we shouldn't and I'll have to remember not to ask you for too much information about your personal life.'

'Good. I hope you can spread the word on that issue if necessary. Now, let's get these drinks distributed, hopefully to the right recipients.'

As she drove home on Friday, Gabriella was happily contemplating a relaxing evening, perhaps a glass of Shiraz with her meal, followed by a hot shower and an early night. Wonderful thoughts for the end of the week. She had worked a bit later than was normal for a Friday and had decided to call at the big, out of town supermarket on the way home as well. Closing the front door, she noticed the light winking on the answer machine, dropped her bags in the hall, and pressed play. She immediately recognised the voice even though he bothered to start by telling her that this was Tom. She listened as he apologised for his absence on Wednesday, explaining that his boss had asked him to attend a meeting in Edinburgh and that's where he was ringing from.

'So I'm really sorry to have missed seeing you and I'm ringing tonight because I have something important to tell you.'

She listened hard, wondering what was so important that he had to ring from Scotland.

'Gabriella, I know this may come as a bit of a shock, but I have to tell you that I think I'm falling in love with you.'

She hardly heard the last bit about when he would be back, but suddenly realised he was giving her his address and asking her to come to his house on Saturday night. He would be home mid-afternoon, might or might not get down to the club, but would be ready for coffee with her at nine.

'Goodnight Gabriella. I love you.'

She replaced the phone and wandered into the kitchen in a daze. This man had no idea what constituted "a bit of a shock." She put the kettle on, made tea, sat at the table and sipped it slowly. What on earth was happening to her usual, orderly life all of a sudden? The rest of the evening passed in a similar daze – so much so that she forgot all about the Shiraz. Climbing the stairs, she walked into the bathroom.

'Oh my word,' she said to her astonished face looking back at her from the mirror, 'where exactly has that come from?'

It was a question she felt needed some thinking through, as rationally as her addled senses could manage. So finally, clean all over, she got into bed and lay down, pulling the duvet up to her chin like a comfort blanket, knowing that sleep would elude her for hours yet. Then she thought back. Their first meetings had thrown up nothing except critical, occasional comment. Then there was the Jason incident, but anyone in the same position as Tom would have reacted with concern and chivalry. Next she got to the surprising invitation to the theatre. It had been a great day out and yes, she had found him different, charming like others had said and good fun to be with. But there had been no hint of anything romantic, she was certain of that. There was, she felt sure, nothing that could have prepared her for this.

And having found no satisfactory answers, the big question remained. What on earth was she going to do on Saturday?

Game, Set and Love Match

CHAPTER 5

Saturday. Crunch time. Household chores were somehow mechanically attempted, and by mid-afternoon, her anxiety decibels were definitely rising. For a few moments, she wondered whether to go or not, but realised that yes, she must. Possibly, by then, she would have an answer to give to this man with the deep blue eyes and the ability to cause seismic shock. In the end, she decided on action: she would get down to the club as early as possible and immerse herself in tennis, knowing that Tom wouldn't be there early - if at all.

And it worked. She had played for over two hours and was just walking off court from her last game, which had been with three people she hardly knew, when she saw him sitting on the bench outside the pavilion. Her heart gave a violent bang and she could feel that awful tightening in the throat as the muscles constricted. Her playing partners peeled away towards the pavilion door and she was left to walk towards him. He stood as she approached, smiling at her.

'Hello, Gabriella.'

She took a deep breath.

'Hello Simon. What brings you back here?'

Sitting down heavily on the bench she wondered what on earth was going on with her usually uncomplicated life.

He sat down beside her.

'An unexpected turn of events actually.'

'Oh.'

Yes, she knew about those.

'It's Brian's Dad. He's not been well for a while and they were intending to have him come and live with them – hence the move to a bigger house. But he's got a lot worse recently and so they thought he ought to move down sooner rather than later. As I had a long weekend off work, I fetched him down yesterday from York, and I'll go back tomorrow. Bit of a long trip, but it helped out.'

'That was very kind. Hope he improves.'

The muscles were beginning to relax now that he had turned out to be here again only as a Good Samaritan.

'Yes, I think he will, now that Sam will be force-feeding him his medication if necessary.'

Gabriella smiled. She could imagine the hapless father-in-law in the care of no-nonsense Sam.

'But, the other thing is that while I was unexpectedly back here, I thought it was a good opportunity to see you.'

Her insides started doing little lurching things as he spoke.

'So I popped down here specially, Gabriella. Can we go to a pub for a drink?'

The expression and the grey eyes, she noted, were both very serious now.

'I do need to talk to you.'

'Need to talk to me?'

She was sounding like a parrot.

'Yes. Is there a pub or somewhere we could go to?'

Her mind was going blank but she suddenly remembered what she was supposed to be doing this Saturday evening.

'I can't. I have an arrangement to go to a friend's for coffee at nine.'

'Half an hour's fine. What about the clubhouse then?'

She was absolutely trapped. There was no reason that Simon or anyone else around them knew that would reasonably prevent her from having a drink with him and she sensed that whatever he had to say needed hearing and dealing with.

'OK. Let me just put my bag in the car first.'

She fetched her bag and walked to her car, her hands shaking so much that she had difficulty with the key-fob. There was no sign of a large, silver car in the car park, but Gabriella couldn't believe how these two events had collided on this one Saturday night. Returning to where Simon was waiting for her, she did her best to look relaxed and normal, while feeling nervous and slightly dizzy.

'Right, let's go.'

As they walked up the path, Simon told her about Sam's new house and the fact that they were hoping to start a family sometime soon. They entered the bar area and Gabriella got drinks, aware that whatever subject of conversation she started, she was almost babbling with barely-suppressed nerves. It was no surprise that he led her to the same table where they had sat before, at the farthest end of the room.

'I need to talk to you.'

'Yes, so you said, what about?'

Now that she had stopped babbling, she could hardly get the words out and tried to sip her drink, holding her glass tightly, hoping her still-trembling hands weren't visible.

'Well, in a few months I need to think about a new contract at work or decide that it's time to quit my job in the North Sea. It's been really great and I've had a fabulous time, enjoyed it immensely.'

He was looking at her very intently and she somehow knew what he was going to say next.

'Gabriella, as I was back here, I wanted to come down , on the off-chance of seeing you and ask whether, if I gave up working on an oil rig in the North Sea and became a respectable land-based engineer, we could get together. So I've come to throw my hat into the ring as it were.'

The grey eyes were still quite serious as he picked up his glass, and continued to look at her. Because somehow she had seen this coming as soon as he had mentioned giving up his job, she was ready to respond.

'Simon, it's very gallant of you to think of giving up your job, on my account, but you mustn't do it, absolutely not.'

He drank for a moment.

'Are you sure? I thought we got on well at first meeting and could have something going for us. As far as I know, you appear not to have anyone else in your life.'

She listened to those words. What irony, tonight of all nights.

'Yes, I'm absolutely sure, Simon.'

She was thinking as quickly as she could, knowing that he would expect reasons and a logical line of argument that an engineer could not fault. She took a quick drink, placed her glass down and looked at him across the table.

'You talk about throwing your hat into the ring. Let me use that to explain my refusal. You see, when a person throws his hat into the ring, I might think it's a nice hat today, but I have to be sure that I'll still like it in ten, twenty or even fifty years' time and that's a big ask and one which I'm not prepared to commit to.'

Simon was not going to let her off that lightly and started to question her about this uncertainty she had expressed about commitment and why that was such a big deal. He spoke passionately, arguing that such unquantifiable doubts were not a reasonable basis for out-and-out refusal. But she held firm, knowing that in the end, she had rejected his idea and he would have to accept it, whether she could explain her reasons to his satisfaction or not. She tried to deflect him from the main topic.

'Suppose I hadn't been here tonight, what would you have done then?'

'I would have got your telephone number from someone so I could contact you. In fact as this may have been a bit of a shock,' Gabriella couldn't believe she was hearing exactly the same words again, it was sounding like a verbal version of Groundhog Day, 'I can ring you tomorrow before I set off to see if you've thought about it and changed your mind.'

She shook her head.

'I obviously can't stop you trying again, but I really would counsel you against it. I'm very certain.'

Then she had another awful thought.

'Does Sam know you're here to see me?'

'No. Well only that I've popped in to say "Hello" in general and have a drink.

Gabriella exhaled in relief. That was good, but what was going on in her life all of a sudden?

* * *

As he left the airport, Tom was feeling both elated and just a bit apprehensive. He realised that as his own feelings had suddenly become clear and he knew he wanted this lovely young woman in his life, his phone message had probably been like some extraordinary bolt from the blue to her. There was, therefore, a slight doubt in his mind. Suppose

Gabriella had thought him barking mad and decided she wanted nothing to do with him? He might get home to a "thanks but no thanks" message on his own answer phone.

The next part of the journey was just as slow and tiresome as he had expected; it was in fact a Bank Holiday weekend and there seemed to be road works silting the whole area around the airport to a halt. Eventually the taxi made it to the station; the train was only fifteen minutes late, Jon was waiting and once home, Tom raced in and checked the phone. No message from her. Excellent.

Feeling buoyed-up by the fact that she hadn't apparently rejected him outright, he sorted out his things, dealt with post, re-checked his phone messages, which included one from his mother in New Zealand telling him that his step-father had broken his leg, and thought about a meal.

Later, showered and changed into casual clothes, he looked at his watch and decided to go for it rather than just sit, waiting. But driving in through the club gates he suddenly felt nervous. He smiled to himself. Bit of a turn up, Tom Scotford, not feeling in control of what's happening around you. He drove slowly past the line of parked cars. A small, yellow convertible was among them. He felt an electric buzz of excitement, or was it nervousness? Getting out of the driver's seat, he took an extra minute sweeping his gaze around the courts looking for Gabriella, but he couldn't see her playing. Good, perhaps she's already finished and is packing up, ready to go. He walked across the tarmac, straightened his back and stepped through the pavilion doorway. The room was empty. He checked his watch, it was eight-forty and as he looked back out of the doorway, he saw people starting to pack up on one of the courts. Mike's teenage son, Kris, had detached himself from the others and was bounding towards him.

'Hi, Kris. Been let out for the evening? What's happened to the revision?'

'Mum said I could have the weekend off.'

He looked accusingly at Tom.

'You should've been here. I've been here since six. We've had some good games.'

'Excellent.'

He saw an opportunity.

'Who've you played with?'

Kris was sitting on a chair, easing his foot out of a trainer.

'Oh, everybody. But Gabriella and I beat George and a woman I don't know,' he volunteered.

'Oh, Gabriella's here somewhere is she?'

He tried to sound totally unconcerned.

'Can't see her.'

'Yeah,' Kris looked up briefly from an inspection of his right big toe, 'she's gone up to the clubhouse with this chap who turned up.'

The words hit him like a blast from a gun.

'What chap who turned up?'

'Dunno. No-one I'd seen before. I think Mum said he'd been down a bit ago. He didn't come to play, just to watch.'

He was forcing his shoe back on, quite oblivious to the effect his words were having.

Tom leaned against the doorjamb, looking out onto the courts but not registering anything. It was surprisingly easy to put those few scraps of information together: a chap had turned up, Kris didn't recognise him, but Su did. Kris had not been at the club much in the last few weeks. It was obvious: Simon had come back for Gabriella.

'Are they coming in yet?'

Kris's voice sounded miles away.

'What? Er, don't know. I mean, no, still chatting.'

He stood, immobile. What was he going to do now for goodness sake?

'I'll check how long the rest are going to be.'

Kris was pushing past him and loping off to the side of the court where Mike was playing. He watched, couldn't hear what was being said, but Kris was returning.

'A few minutes,' he announced, 'what's the time?'

'Quarter to nine.'

Kris was staring out at the courts.

'Shall we go up to the clubhouse? Beat the rush to the bar?'

Tom nodded. He needed to get up there, see for himself what was going on and Kris was as good a person to go with as any, being totally unaware of any sub-plot that was emerging. He could see other players starting to pack up now.

When they entered, he made himself walk straight to the bar and get their drinks, but while he was waiting for them, glanced casually towards the end of the room. It was an identical tableau to the one he had previously seen – a young couple sitting on either side of the table from each other, talking. He didn't continue to look, but followed Kris across the room to where the group who had just come off court were starting to gather. As he had got Kris a drink, he automatically asked the others if he could get theirs, as usual. He was quite surprised that Mike stepped forward.

'No, Tom, not your turn, I'll get them.'

He managed to position himself on the edge of the group and, in answer to the inevitable question, told them he had just come back from working in Scotland. That set off a round of tales about holidays north of the Border and the Edinburgh Tattoo and Festival. He drank his half of beer, willing himself not to turn round and look down the room. Then the conversation suddenly changed.

'I see that young man Simon is back,' he heard Alice remark.

Sliding further backwards, he asked Kris some inane question about his forthcoming exams and managed to look as though he was really interested in the answer. He was about to ask something else, when, to his astonishment, Simon himself was joining their group. He half listened as people started to ask him why he was here again, vaguely heard the words "House" and "Father" mentioned and wished he could now get out of the corner he was wedged in and see where Gabriella was standing.

'What's happened to Gabriella, is she coming back for a drink?' Mike was asking.

Simon shook his head.

'No she had to meet a friend at nine o'clock, so she's gone.'

He then continued to answer a question about his sister and Tom switched off and drank a few more gulps of beer. Suddenly the words blazed into his consciousness, "she's gone to meet a friend at nine o'clock." It hit him like a thunderbolt. Hell that means me, she's gone to meet me. He pulled his phone from his pocket, looked at it and announced to the group in general, whether they were listening or not, 'Sorry, folks, need to get home and sort something.' Waving the phone as though it had just imparted this news, he started moving away from the table.

'Hope to have less on next week and be able to play a bit more. Sorry to dash. Bye.'

He pushed the swing door, crossed the lobby, exited the clubhouse and broke into a run. He was half way home, doing forty-five in a thirty zone when he told himself to slow down and concentrate.

Pulling into his drive and braking to an abrupt halt, he saw Gabriella's car parked in front of the steps to the house. He walked over, anxiety, nervousness, hope, all sorts of emotions crowding in as he opened her car door. She looked up at him from the driver's seat.

'You'll be getting cold, come in and let me make a hot drink.'

She started to ease out of the seat.

'I'm OK. I put on my tracksuit and I've only been here about five minutes, but I'd love a cup of tea please.'

He ushered her in, suddenly realising that this was the first time she had been in his house. Nervousness, worse than when he'd driven into the club earlier on, started to grip him. He motioned towards rooms as they passed on the way to the kitchen and then seeing that she had gravitated to the table and chairs at the far end, busied himself with the tea. There was a pause, both seemingly bereft of conversation. The only noise was the kettle boiling. Gabriella had walked to the patio doors and was studiously looking out at the garden; he was now pouring tea. The silence was almost tangible. He cleared his throat, about to hand her the mug.

'I don't know whether you have sugar in tea. I don't think you had it in coffee when we went to the theatre.'

He paused distractedly.

'That seems ages ago now.'

She shook her head to decline any sugar, took the mug and cupped her hands round it, giving him a thoughtful look.

'You mean a lot of water has suddenly gone under your bridge?'

He sat down at the table.

'Yes, especially in the last half hour or so.'

She drew in a deep breath and nodded imperceptibly.

'I'd better tell you what happened. I presume you want to hear it?'

'Yes, please. You do know how cold it can get in Aberdeen, don't you?'

The lame joke was all he could manage to ease the tension, but he saw a flicker of a smile. Then, she told him briefly about Simon's arrival, his insistence that they talked, that he was thinking of quitting his job and would do so, if she would agree to start seeing him.

'Oh.'

He'd been right about Simon coming back because of her, but he hadn't remotely thought he would be offering to give up his job as well.

'So, a big thing to consider.'

'In some ways, yes.'

'And how did you consider it?'

He needed to ask the question but honestly didn't think he wanted to hear the answer. He remembered thinking they were together earlier in May and now, it seemed, they might be. She looked at him and he was amazed that she seemed quite calm, more so than he felt, he thought. He reached for his mug, needing to do something.

'I told him that he mustn't do that on my account.'

'You did?'

The words sounded almost joyful and his mug banged back down on the table.

'But I thought you quite liked him, you seemed upset that night when he left.'

She nodded.

'Yes, I was attracted to him initially, he was friendly and easy going, but he left without making any arrangement for us to keep in contact and I listened carefully to the words he used tonight and I wasn't impressed by their sincerity, even though he seemed to be making a very serious proposition.'

Tom felt totally perplexed.

'Words? Why, what words? What did he say?'

'Well, he talked about coming to see me "on the off-chance," as though it was merely a spur of the moment decision and he put his proposition in terms of "throwing his hat into the ring." That gives the impression of just trying something out to see what might happen, if you like. But when he talked of his job, the language was very specific, he thought it was "fabulous," it was clearly important in his life and I wondered what would happen if he gave it all up and then regretted that decision when life became a bit more humdrum and less challenging. Yes, he'd come into my life briefly, but it hadn't taken me long, I realised, to forget him once he had walked out.'

'Did you tell him that was why you were refusing him?'

'Not really, I concentrated on overturning his idea of throwing his hat into the ring.'

She explained what she meant and what she had told Simon, and he noted that her argument was based on not wanting to make a long term commitment. That sounded like an awful stumbling block. He guessed that might account for the fact that this very lovely young girl was still very unattached.

'Did he accept that?'

'Well, he really had no choice. He says he might try to ring me tomorrow to see if I've changed my mind, but I told him that wouldn't happen.'

There was a pause as she drank some more tea.

'So, having disposed of one bus, I now have to turn to the second.'

'Bus?'

He hadn't a clue what she was now talking about.

'Well it occurred to me that having waited some time for one boyfriend to turn up, two appear simultaneously, like buses are supposed to do.'

He started to laugh. This girl had such a quirky, original mind, that was one of the reasons he knew he loved her. But her words brought him back to his phone call and he became serious again.

'So, what are you going to do about this one? When I gave you a chance to think about having me in your life, I'd no idea you were going to end up with a choice of two of us.'

She smiled.

'You said it would be a shock, and it was. I honestly didn't see it coming and have tried to see whether I missed something obvious, but couldn't see that either. Then the sight of Simon was a second shock, but I really didn't treat it as a choice between the two of you. Although I once thought he was a nice guy, when it came to the crunch moment, I knew instinctively that Simon wasn't right for me.'

She paused again and then looked directly at him.

'And so I now have to tell you what I thought about you.'

He sat still, heart thudding against his ribs, mouth dry despite the tea. She had rejected Simon and he felt that he was likely to go the same way. The kitchen was absolutely silent, as though it too was holding its breath.

'I haven't known you long and so all I could do was look at the few times we had been together and see what it had been like.'

He thought cold water was being poured over him, remembering what she had told him about her first impressions.

'First impressions I think I could discount, as for some reason, we just seemed to get off on the wrong foot.'

He relaxed a bit in relief.

'Then you helped with the Jason incident which was probably only as much as anyone would have done, but you did it and you seemed genuinely kind and considerate when you rang. So that left our day out and on that occasion you had been good company, fun to be with and increasingly more relaxed. More like the charming Tom Scotford the others had told me about. '

She looked at him and he could tell that the next sentence was going to clinch it one way or the other.

'Tom, I know I'm not in love with you.'

She must have seen the anguished expression flood over his face as she held up her hand.

'Listen. But, I'm prepared to start going on a journey with you, I would really like to get to know you, go out with you and see how far we get and where it might lead. That's all I can offer you tonight and I'm prepared for you to say it's not enough. But I would really like to try and see how things go.'

She sat back in her chair and, for the first time, looked anxious and tired herself. Tom felt waves of relief, elation and tiredness sweeping through him as he reached across the table and took her hand.

'Gabriella, thank you. It's enough, it's fabulous. We're going to have such a good time, you'll see. I promise you.'

She just nodded.

'Well, let's try. You'll have to be patient; I go slowly with things and test them out. You'll probably want to go much faster.'

'Don't care. I can be patient. I can be whatever you want.'

He was now soaring, exultant.

'Um, rash promises Tom Scotford.'

But she was smiling at him.

'And now, I'm absolutely whacked and need to go home.'

'Yes, being run over, metaphorically, by two buses takes it out of you.'

He could joke now.

'We'll talk more tomorrow and sometime I'll try to explain why I suddenly realised what a beautiful young lady you are and why I should do something about it.'

She nodded as though that would be a good thing to hear, rose and started to pick up her bag from the chair. But he reached out, took it from her and replaced it.

'Gabriella,' he moved towards her, folded her in his arms, 'before you go, I've got to kiss you, I so want to do this.'

She looked up at him as his mouth closed over her lips. The electric, explosive sensation that ripped through her was entirely new and she understood that phrase, "he took my breath away." Releasing her from the tightness of his grasp, he continued to hold her. A little smile played round her mouth as she looked up into that handsome face and those amazing eyes.

'Gosh, I think I might have made a good decision.'

That was enough encouragement and they kissed again, and then again. Finally he let her step back, retrieve her bag and he put his arm round her as they made for the front door. When she was settled in her car, he leaned in and kissed her lightly.

'Sleep well, my darling girl. I'll ring you in the morning, about ten and we'll talk about starting out on this journey.'

'Goodnight Tom, sweet dreams. Yes, we'll talk tomorrow.'

CHAPTER 6

On Sunday Gabriella woke feeling that life was suddenly turning into a series of totally unexpected events. She wondered if Simon might ring, not that it mattered, but she couldn't tell him about Tom because she wanted, as far as possible, to keep their new relationship private. Quite how, they would have to discuss and work out.

Tom rang and asked if she would come over for a meal, immediately if she could. She had laughed at his desire to start on their journey as quickly as possible, told him she had jobs to do and would be there mid-afternoon at the earliest. He had said he thought he could just wait that long! She had laughed at him and told him the hours would pass quickly enough, he would find. But as she did those jobs and tried to fill in the time that she had insisted on, she too wondered if it had been a mistake to wait so long before seeing him again.

And as she prepared to go over to his house and have a meal together, she began to realise just how little they knew about each other. Closing her front door, she got into her car and drove, for the second time in twenty-four hours, to Number 8 The Avenue. Driving through the outskirts of town, she was surprised to find that she could hardly remember anything about the house from last night's visit, except that they had sat in the kitchen which had a patio door looking out onto the garden. I must have been in a bit of a state, she thought, still not being able to harness any reasonable memories at all.

The gravel spat from beneath her tyres as she turned into the circular drive in front of his house. Number 8 was not as large as some in the road, but well proportioned, plainly built and, she decided, just the sort of house she might have imagined Tom would live in. Looking at it now in daylight, she noted a double, detached garage and to the right a stone, gated archway with rambler roses flopping untidily over it. Switching off the ignition, she climbed the steps to the front door, which was hurled open before she could ring the bell. Once in the hall he was kissing her and telling her this was the start of their journey and he would do anything to make it as fabulous for her as he had promised. She laughed, carried away by his enthusiasm, wondering just how this was all going to work out. She was an analyst, after all, and so far this had defied analysis or rational explanation.

'Now I really need to look at this house again as I've virtually no recollection of what it was like.'

'Well, you were in a state of double shock, so perhaps it's not that surprising.' Ushering her through the hall, pointing out rooms again as they passed, he led her back into the kitchen. This time she was trying to take it all in.

'Oh, what a nice room.'

Gabriella was looking around at the Shaker-style cabinets, granite work surfaces, vaguely remembering the light wooden table and chairs in front of the patio doors. She saw him smile and look pleased by her words. She knew that showing off one's home was quite a personal thing to do, but so far the house had passed its first examinations.

'Do you mind the kitchen? We can go into the sitting room if you'd rather.'

'No, no. This is absolutely fine.'

She sat at the table, interested to start learning things about him.

'Was it like this when you bought the house or have you had it done?'

'I had it re-done, making it slightly larger to get the table in at one end and I had the door put in. That meant a smaller dining room, but I thought it would suit me better this way.'

'Yes, it's a good use of space and these doors to the garden are just so nice. Do you sit out when you can?'

'Yes, I do and I love it. We've had good weather recently. We can go out and sit for a while if you'd like.'

His words tailed off and both seemed to recognise that their conversation was a little formal – neither was yet at ease with the other.

She was looking out at the garden and then turned with a slightly puzzled expression.

'Can I ask you a personal question?'

He looked a bit taken aback, but nodded.

'Yes, yes, of course you can. You can ask me anything.'

'You really live here on your own?'

'Yes. Why do you ask?'

His tone suggested that he wondered what on earth had prompted that.

'Well, this is a lovely kitchen and it's all beautifully clean and tidy, so how do you manage?'

He threw his head back and laughed. Some of the formality seemed to melt away.

'So, you don't think I can be clean and tidy Gabriella Devonshire?'

And before she could respond, added, 'I cheat.'

Now she was laughing.

'Obviously. How?'

He explained that a Scottish lady, a widow named Mrs MacClelland, came in twice a week and did whatever needed doing and as he was away all day, things didn't seem to get too bad the rest of the time.

'I have ready meals in the freezer and can manage to re-heat those and do tend to eat out a lot, so I don't do much real cooking I'm afraid. So, we shall be re-heating something tonight, or we can go out if you'd rather.'

'No, eating in's fine. Today is Gabriella-and-Tom-start-to-get-to-know-each-other-a-bit-better day.'

'Wonderful idea. Come on, my lovely lady, let's go into the sitting room, then.'

And he pulled her up.

Settled on one of the large sofas, the main topic of conversation centred on what they were going to do about the tennis club. Gabriella was adamant that she valued her private life highly enough to want to keep their relationship just that.

'So, we just continue as we are. We come and go separately and I will make strenuous efforts not to indulge in any public displays of affection – but you mustn't be cross with me if I fail! Like this,' he added as he kissed her.

Gabriella laughed.

'OK let's try and see how long we can get away with it for.'

And the journey began. They did manage to keep each other at arm's length at the club and as they only got down about twice a week, it wasn't too difficult. On Friday evening, they had coffee together, reviewed Week One and decided that a second week could probably be managed. Tom was privately hoping that Week Two might lead to some more interesting explorations on his part, but he still sensed that Gabriella was going to take her time getting to know Tom Scotford and neither participating in any sort of steamy wrestling match nor even getting acquainted with the master bedroom was on her agenda. Ah well, patience is a virtue and all that.

As she was preparing to leave, Tom remembered they hadn't finally decided what to do tomorrow.

'Where am I going to take you tomorrow?'

'Ah. Nowhere.'

'What? I thought we said...'

'You're not taking me anywhere, I'm taking you.'

She grinned at his amazed expression.

'I'll pick you up at twelve, and wear sensible shoes; we're going for a walk, amongst other things.'

'No, this isn't right. You shouldn't be...'

'Do you want to come or not?'

'Of course I do.'

He was totally unable to respond to her independence.

'I'm just not used to...'

'Well, it's a new experience for you.'

She kissed him, smiling up at him, enjoying the moment, enjoying his discomfort.

'Twelve noon. Be ready.'

Just before twelve Gabriella arrived and was about to switch off the engine when the front door opened and Tom appeared, dressed, she immediately noted, in blue jeans, almost an exact match to the ones she was wearing. His short-sleeved shirt was a very pale, washed-out blue and looked so casual that it had to be mega-expensive while at least her tee shirt was cream, or they would have looked cloned. He opened the passenger door.

'Taxi for Mr Scotford,' she grinned at him as he stretched his legs into the front seat-well, 'are you ready for your adventure?'

'Looking forward to it immensely.'

He leaned over and kissed her.

'Let's go.'

'It'll take us about twenty minutes to get there; we'll eat first and then do a walk if you like. We're going to a canal and there's a lock about half a mile down the towpath which is good to sit by and watch the boats.'

'Fabulous, darling, you can be my event organiser anytime.'

'Wait out a bit, you may hate it and the chef might be having a bad hair day.'

He laughed and while she drove, started to ask about what she'd been doing at work, and after she'd given him a quick precis, was about to tell her a bit about his own week when she became obviously preoccupied with the demands of driving or rather navigating.

'Now,' Gabriella was concentrating on where to turn off, 'I think we turn down here although it looks like a dead end, because it is or you fall in the canal. So you're about to find out where you're going because there's the sign and that's it at the end of this lane.'

They drew up in front of "The Jolly Boatman" which was just as its name suggested. The doors and windows were thrown open and there was a lively babble of conversation from a variety of customers, many of whom had obviously just moored up on the canal and come for a drink or a meal. There were wooden tables and benches scattered haphazardly on a piece of grass which bordered the towpath and people were negotiating their various ways among them, shouting greetings to each other and carrying pints of beer or bottles of wine. Two waiters in long, green aprons were scurrying about, taking orders and appearing with trays loaded with food.

'This looks great, what a lively atmosphere.'

Tom threw an arm round her shoulders as they walked towards the door.

'Great choice, I know I'm going to enjoy this.'

They found a table, and ordered mineral water for "the driver" and a beer for Tom.

'Now,' Gabriella was opening her menu, 'let's see what they have to offer. The fish, non-canal variety, is usually good.'

Tom had glanced at his menu and then suddenly closed it. Gabriella looked at him.

'Don't you want to eat?'

'Yes, but you can choose for me, please.'

'No, no I can't. I know nothing of your likes and dislikes yet. No.'

She was looking surprisingly worried.

'It's easy. I like anything and everything. I'm really not a fussy eater. Honestly. I eat cheese sandwiches sometimes in the evening. You can't go wrong.'

She was still looking terribly doubtful.

'Trust me. There's nothing to worry about.'

'You'll find that I do worry quite a lot,' she said quietly.

'No need, most of the time. I'll teach you not to.'

'Alright, that would be good,' then glancing briefly at the menu, 'you're going to have the goat's cheese and beetroot starter followed by one of their specials. We shall have paella.'

She motioned to a passing waiter and placed their order.

'Fabulous. So, no more worries about food, right?'

She nodded but then fixed him with a quizzical look.

'But you have a responsible job. You must worry about that at times.'

He thought for a moment.

'I think I'd say that I'm conscientious enough to ensure I do a good job and I'd only worry if I thought I hadn't done my best or if things were slipping out of my control for some reason.'

'Oh, right.'

She mulled this over.

'So what does stress you out?'

'Not a lot really. I'm an optimist, so if things aren't going well at the time, I always believe there will be an upturn.'

'Gosh, I don't think I could be quite as laid-back about life as that, so what do you do when...'

She was unable to finish her question as a waiter arrived with their starters.

As he ate, Tom tucked that bit of information away and determined that he would try his best to stop her worrying about what he was sure would be pretty insignificant stuff. His food was excellent and he was beginning to like this place a lot. He gazed around and took in the surroundings. The pub's interior was quite plain with pale yellow walls, some exposed stone, wooden floorboards and no canned music. It was lively without being noisy and the plates of food being carried from the kitchen looked enormous. They talked sporadically as they ate and he discovered they were both only children and each declared they would have liked a sibling sister.

'Gabriella, can I ask you a personal question?'

She looked up, uneasily.

'Erm, yes.'

'How old are you?'

'Tom, don't you know you're not supposed to ask a lady her age?'

Then as he started to apologise, 'I'm twenty-eight. You?'

'Thirty seven.'

Um, quite well preserved then!'

And they laughed but then he was disappointed to learn he couldn't look forward to buying her a present as her birthday was in April.

And, having demolished his starter, he was really looking forward to the paella as he realised that yet again he was having a wonderful day out with this gorgeous girl, who might, just might, soon be totally his.

'So,' Gabriella put down her knife and fork, 'talking of work, did someone say you'd recently been to Amsterdam?'

'Yes, only for a day to see people in our satellite office there and just check up on a few things. But it was a good trip, everything was going well and I have a good friend and colleague there which makes it even more enjoyable.'

He told her about Vim, who managed the office, and spent some time recounting one or two of their more hair-raising nights out, particularly one in Singapore.

'So did you and Vim have a naughty night out in Amsterdam?'

He laughed.

'No, I came back to London and had a very sober night in the hotel.'

He was now struggling with what to say next. Was he going to tell her about the next night in London? He was saved from a decision by the arrival of their waiter to clear the plates.

'Starters were excellent, tell the chef.'

'Thank you sir, I will.'

Gabriella looked at him and smiled, not knowing if he were telling the truth or trying to bolster her confidence. But, she had to agree, the food had been really good.

'Now, you tell me a bit more about your colleagues, especially Steve. Is he a good boss to work for?'

He wanted to find out as much as he could about her, what she thought of people and situations. What made her tick. Gabriella sat back in her chair, topped up her glass and gave him some pen-portraits of her colleagues and confirmed that Steve was both an excellent boss and also a good friend. Tom noted that she could paint amusing pictures in words and spoke about the people with genuine warmth. Then, she saw the waiter approaching.

'Now I think we must get ready for more food.'

Tom looked up and saw a large iron pan being transported from the kitchen and borne towards their table. It was the paella.

'Please take care, the dish is very hot. Enjoy your meal.'

They really didn't need an invitation to start and there was silence as they attacked the pan, piling food onto their plates. Then an even more lengthy silence enveloped them both. Conversation was disjointed as they ate; the food was so good it had to take precedence.

'That was amazingly good.'

Tom sat back, a pile of bones and shells in a bowl beside his plate.

'I can't remember the last time I had paella and that was wonderful.'

He was thinking as he spoke of all the cordon-bleu meals he had consumed over the last few years, but this had been both a total surprise and a great taste.

'And before you ask, no, I can't manage anything else, except a coffee.'

'I'm glad you enjoyed it and we'll have coffee. Then we'll have to walk some of it off.'

'Suits me. Did you say there was a lock nearby?'

Gabriella nodded and when the plates had been cleared and the coffees ordered, sauntered off to the Ladies.

Tom heaved a contented sigh. He had forgotten how to enjoy excellent pub food and this was so different from his normal meals out. They also seemed to be getting to grips with the getting-to-know-you bit as well. As they had talked, he had noted the guarded way in which she dealt with some personal questions, but was fine with non-personal chitchat, and that intrigued him to find out more about her and her background. He had a distinct feeling that he just might be starting to steer his life in a totally new direction and that was very exciting. He was about to continue exploring that direction when Gabriella returned, but the coffee was on the table and he could wait a while, no real hurry at all.

After the coffee jug had been emptied, Gabriella looked at him.

'Right, best foot forward as they say.'

She stood and started for the door.

Tom hesitated.

'But no one's brought a bill yet.'

'All done,' she laughed at his shocked expression, 'you're free to leave the premises.' She was almost at the door, shouting thanks to the staff. He rose, adding his thanks as he went and caught her up outside.

'You shouldn't have done that. This...this is awful.'

'Don't fret, Tom. You'll have to get used to the fact that I'm pretty used to my independence and have no intention of giving it up just because we're going out together.'

She stopped on the path and turned to face him, putting on her stern expression that really wasn't.

'I've noticed you tend always to pick up the tab for people and they sort of let you, because, well, they know you can. But it doesn't mean you should have to. Come on, don't tell me you're totally shocked to have a woman pay for your lunch.'

She was now grinning again at his renewed discomfiture.

'I am shocked, but I'll say thank you. A surprise I really didn't expect.'

They had got to the towpath and started to walk. It was a hot day now, almost too hot and they walked, often in single file, along the narrow path, occasionally stopping to admire a butterfly's dazzling wings or greet people coming in the opposite direction. Tom was still muttering about the novelty of someone paying for his lunch when Gabriella turned to face him.

'Look, a bit further on, can you see the lock-keeper's cottage?'

He nodded and they both quickened their pace, eager to get there and see if anything was happening. The lock was empty and they settled onto a seat alongside a little flower bed.

'Oh, Salvias,' Gabriella was inspecting the flowers a bit more closely, 'one plant I really dislike, too red, too upright, too formal.'

They sat in silence for a while, he had his arm round her shoulders, insects were buzzing drowsily among the flowers, a bird was singing, invisible but happy, and it was all very calm, very peaceful, very English. Tom, who had been making a mental note to ask Ken, his gardener, whether he had any Salvias in his flower beds, was now keen to see what else he could find out and remembered asking her previously about her arrival back at the club. Despite the fact that it had thrown up her initial impression of him, he thought it was ground he could cover from a different angle, or at least different timescale. He recalled someone telling him that Jason had, first time around, been her tennis partner. Presumably he had been a more amenable young man in those days, so he wondered if he had been a boyfriend as well.

'Tell me about your time in Upton Peploe when you first lived here.'

He had thought that was a reasonably innocuous request and was amazed when Gabriella's face changed, she turned towards him, features clouded, no longer the smiling girl with whom he had just had lunch. Her voice was level, her gaze expressionless after that first fleeting cloud.

'I imagined that when I came back, someone at the club would have told you about my earlier life.'

He was shocked by the response, taken aback.

'No, no one talks about you except to say what a lovely young lady you are.'

He was feeling anxious, wondering how on earth he had stumbled into…he didn't know what. But she continued to look calmly at him.

'Oh, it's nothing terrible, just folks seem to find it a bit sad, that's all.'

He was aware that the heat seemed to have got terribly oppressive; there was a sticky, thundery feeling in the air. He could feel sweat trickling down his spine.

'Will you tell me? I'd rather hear your story from you than pick up bits as idle chitchat. But if you'd rather not, it's really OK.'

Although he thought he was speaking quietly, his voice sounded loud in his ears against the absolute stillness around them. Now he was cursing himself for his vacuous inquisitiveness.

'Yes, I'll tell you. And now I think about it, probably only George and Alice would know; all the others are too new.'

She folded her hands in her lap and gazing out across the brown water of the canal, speaking softly, Gabriella was seemingly dredging the memories from a place where they were normally hidden.

'Just two things, really. Firstly, my father was a bit of an alcoholic and my mother died when I was fourteen, leaving Dad to bring me up.'

He exhaled, not being quite prepared for that.

'Gabriella, I'm so sorry. I had no idea.'

She was right; it had made him terribly sad. He wanted to put both arms round her as though to protect her now, but he sensed she didn't seem to want comfort, as she continued to speak quite calmly.

'Please, don't worry. It's in the past and as you can see, I've survived.'

He wondered at what cost and couldn't help himself asking the next questions.

'But how did you cope? Who was there for you, I mean, you were quite young?'

'Oh, I don't think I was so young really. A teenager should be able to get on with most things and in fact I coped because we basically each lived our separate lives. Dad went to work, I went to school and when I came home I would cook our meal, eat mine, leave his keeping warm and shut myself away in my room. My bedroom was my absolute safe haven.'

His mind was reeling with another thought and a flashback to that night in the clubhouse lobby.

'Was your Dad ever violent towards you?'

He saw the image of her swinging an arm in self defence when the drunken Jason had accosted her.

'No, he was one of the maudlin, happy drunks and part of the time he was sober enough to hold down his job and behave like a responsible citizen. But I know that the Jason incident really upset George because he'd sort of warned me that Jason was back and drinking heavily as he probably thought someone else doing that might be a reminder for me.'

She seemed to have read his thoughts. Tom had imagined George was only thinking about the club's reputation, he had no idea that he would have been doubly upset by Jason's drunken brawling. He did pull his arm more closely round her, needing to try to show his love and his sadness.

'The other thing I did to mitigate the home situation was to join the tennis club. I can't remember how it happened, possibly the sports teacher was trying to recruit for them, I don't know. But I joined. It was a way of getting out of the house and I enjoyed it. So largely by keeping out of each other's way, we managed to rub along. I also coped because I knew that I was good enough at school to go to University and that was my passport to my own life.'

'So from the age of fourteen, you learnt to be self-sufficient, make your own decisions and live life on your terms?'

She nodded, still gazing out across the canal.

'Yes, I suppose so. I went to Uni and even,' she half turned towards him and gave him a brief, slightly challenging look, 'you may be surprised to hear, played tennis as part of their team. Once I had left, I felt I had no reason to come back to Upton Peploe.'

'But you're here now. How did that happen?'

'By a rather strange route actually. After Uni, I got my first job in South Wales and it was while I was working there that I heard my father had died. His death didn't surprise me even though he was no great age, so I came back, arranged the funeral, settled up his few affairs and then went back to work.'

He could hardly believe that this was another blow she had suffered, whose consequences she had needed to deal with on her own.

'So you still didn't come back at that point?'

'No. But a year or so later, I thought I needed to move on, saw the job with Steve's firm advertised, got it and was a bit surprised to find I had come full circle. The rest you sort of know.'

He didn't speak for a moment, digesting this. He thought he was beginning to understand something about how her upbringing might have shaped her responses to things and wanted to gauge whether she believed it had.

'This may be a naïve question, but what sort of effect did this actually have on you? You say you've survived and certainly that's very true, but they were traumatic events in a young person's life, and such events do tend to shape us in some way or another.'

She thought for a moment.

'As you said, I learnt self-sufficiency from a reasonably early age and I think,' her voice became quieter as though this next bit was of more significance, 'I guess it made me a bit wary of life in general.'

She paused again as though weighing things up afresh, then looked at him with a slow smile.

'But honestly, no real damage I think. Oh, look,' she was pointing up the canal, 'a narrow boat, great, we can see it through the lock. Go down to the lock-gates, they sometimes like a hand.'

Tom rose from the bench, glad to move, glad that the conversation wouldn't automatically turn to his trouble-free upbringing. He was suddenly aware of how little he knew about Gabriella. He had seen her as a beautiful, feisty young lady, giving as good as she got, sometimes stopping George's bombast in its tracks. But now he thought about it, he had also seen her beat herself up if she got something wrong and at other times become fiercely competitive. In the pub he had seen anxiety. Now he had seen a flash of vulnerability, which was quickly hidden, and he wondered what else there was to know, what else to find out. But, he was learning one uncomfortable truth: life had made Gabriella Devonshire a pretty independent young woman, used to running her own affairs, and one who might not see much reason to change any of that.

Tom had a quick lesson in narrow boating and enjoyed helping move the enormous wooden gates before the lock was filled and the boat was quietly gliding away. He turned back to the seat where Gabriella was still sitting. She seemed perfectly composed as she watched the boat disappear down the canal.

'So do you know all about locks and narrow boats now?'

The sunny, happy lunch-time girl was back.

'More than I did; it looks great, I think I might be hooked on the idea.'

She laughed.

'You realise we missed a trick? We could have begged a lift back to the "Boatman," but now,' she stood up, 'we'll just have to walk.'

As is often usual, the return journey seemed much quicker than the outward one had been and when they got back, the pub was still busy.

'I'm a bit thirsty, and as their beer is so good, I'd like another drink. Can I get something for you as well?'

Gabriella nodded.

'An apple juice would be fine, thanks.'

She moved to one of the benches and sat while Tom disappeared inside. Wondering if the couple in the boat had stopped, she glanced around, but couldn't see them. She remembered a holiday while she was a student when six of them had chartered a narrow boat for a week. Gosh,

I haven't recalled that for years; this dredging the past is making all sorts of stuff re-surface. What could she remember about it? Hmm, yes, it had rained most of the time and they seemed always to have run out of food. Suddenly, horrified and yet wanting to giggle, she recalled the afternoon when herself and Dale, a red-haired science student, had been left on the boat while the others went for provisions and they had engaged in an hour of fumbling sex. She remembered graphically their gaucheness but mostly how she had been mesmerised by the vivid colour of his hair, all of it.

'Here you are.'

The sound of his voice made her jump.

'Sorry. What were you thinking about?'

Tom was putting a glass down on the table.

'Thanks. I was thinking about narrow boats actually.'

She smiled up into his face and noted the blonde hair. A far cry from Dale, she thought with a slow smile - a very far cry - a fair-haired man who hadn't an ounce of gaucheness about him and, she imagined, would probably be very, very good at... She picked up her glass and drank.

CHAPTER 7

Gabriella was sitting, bare feet curled beneath her, on the end of the large sofa in Tom's sitting room. It was eight-thirty, Friday evening and lashing with rain. The book she had open was lying in her lap, having re-read parts of Chapter 5, she had given up and was thinking. Or rather, she had been recalling the events of the weeks since "Seismic Saturday" as it had been dubbed.

They had begun their journey, at first rather hesitantly, trying too hard to be the person each thought the other wanted and then, realising that they must just be themselves. Days out had continued to be great fun. Tom was an excellent organiser and the merest germ of an idea would immediately become reality and he would take her off to the theatre or to a restaurant or gallery. Gabriella knew the local area better than he did and would arrange days out, like the first one to the "Boatman," when she would drive and pay - much to Tom's amazement - until she forced him to realise that she was still one very independent lady.

He worried her with the intensity of his feelings and, as she had predicted, wanted the relationship to go forward much, much faster than she was ready for. It was a wonderful sensation being in his arms, kissing him, but there were boundaries he was having, reluctantly she suspected, to observe, mainly to do with the amount of her clothing he could remove and whether she would sleep with him. Answer no. But, he did observe this, and they were getting to know each other, getting used to each other and, surprisingly, managing to keep their romance secret from the tennis club fraternity. And with Tom trying desperately hard not to engage in any public displays of affection despite one narrow squeak, when he had bounded into the pavilion and kissed her just before Alice had walked through the door, they had survived.

'I don't see many pages being turned in that book.'

Tom was sitting almost opposite closing down his laptop and looking at her with an amused expression.

'I'm thinking about what I've just read. No, that's not true, I'm just thinking. Have you finished your work?'

'Yes.'

He had come home slightly earlier than he usually did and after they had eaten, had wanted just to finish off some notes and bring his calendar up to date. The last thing he had done was to delete his August leave dates and reinstate them as office days. That had made him think about holidays, but he was quite sure it was too early to broach that yet, especially as it would throw up the question of sleeping arrangements. Well he had boasted that he could be patient and he was jolly well going to have to be by the look of things. But it would be worth it, he was really, really certain of that. He stretched and stood up.

'Do you want a drink? I think I need a coffee.'

'Yes please. And we need to talk about what we're going to do tomorrow. Tennis - weather permitting - or something different?'

'Something different if you don't mind. I'd like to go shopping.'

'That sounds good. Do you have somewhere in mind?'

Of course he did. And he knew what he wanted to buy.

He bent down and kissed her.

'We'll have a great day out and can play tennis in the evening, or not. See how we feel. And now, I'll make those drinks.'

* * *

'Good weekend?'

It was Monday morning and Steve had sauntered into her office and settled into a chair while he drank a cup of coffee.

'Yes, really nice thanks.'

'Did the new man whisk you off somewhere special?'

She laughed.

'No, we went shopping for a jacket which he wanted. And he found one that he liked, so that was OK.'

'And what did you buy or did he treat you?'

She paused as though weighing up the next bit.

'Well he wanted to buy me something, but I wouldn't let him.'

'Not a diamond ring by any chance?'

He was grinning at her, winding her up.

'Gracious no. He seemed to have this thing about wanting to buy me a designer handbag.'

'And you refused?'

She nodded.

'Yes, they were hundreds and hundreds of pounds. I mean no-one should pay that sort of money for a handbag. So I wouldn't let him.'

Steve let out a slow whistle.

'Would you come and teach my wife the art of saying no to handbags, and coats and shoes?'

Now it was Gabriella's turn to grin.

'I'm sure Julie knows what she wants and also knows what's good value for money and what isn't.'

Steve rose from his chair.

'Well, sometimes she does,' he conceded, 'but, if Tom wants to lavish a handbag on anyone, I'm sure she'd say yes.'

He left and Gabriella sat for a moment, re-living the shopping trip. She had been totally surprised at the urgency with which Tom had tried to persuade her to have a bag and the fact that he had seemed almost upset that she had so flatly refused. In the end, she had found a purse she had liked and he had been delighted to buy that. After they had got back from the shopping mall, he had dropped her at her cottage and then later they had each turned up at, and eventually left the club quite separately, knowing they would have all day Sunday to just laze about, share food and talk. Which is exactly what they had done. He had told her about his mother, now re-married and living in New Zealand and about his stepfather who had broken his leg. She had wondered, but hadn't asked, why the first marriage had similarly broken. Then he had given her a hilarious account of his rather scatty, Bohemian father who now lived in France and "dabbled" in art and antiques. Gabriella had thought he sounded good fun but perhaps had been a bit too difficult for his mother to live with. She smiled, remembering it all, fitting in more bits of the Tom Scotford jigsaw. Then she wondered what Tom would be like to live with. She thought he was easy-going but would put his foot down if necessary. In fact, she conjectured, he would probably be easier to live with than she would. Not a topic to be pursued at the moment though, she reminded herself. So, all in all, a very nice weekend, just as she had said.

When her phone rang on Tuesday night, only moments after Gabriella had got out of the shower, she could hear the excitement in Tom's voice. His words came tumbling out as he told her that he had been asked, at very short notice, to go to a conference in place of a colleague who had been taken ill. Gabriella couldn't really imagine why he was so excited about this.

'And the great thing is, the conference is in Rome, so I've booked you a seat on the plane and your own room in the hotel where the conference is being held.'

Gabriella couldn't quite believe what she was now hearing.

'You've done what?'

'It's all arranged. It'll be short notice as we leave very early on Thursday but I know Steve will let you go and we can do the sights and some shopping as I needn't go to all the sessions. It'll be like a mini holiday. We'll have a great time.'

'No, no we won't Tom...' she couldn't finish the sentence.

'Yes, yes, we will, it'll be fabulous, it's too good an opportunity to turn down. So, just agree and pack a bag.'

'Tom, I'm sorry, but I have no intention of just agreeing and packing a bag. I'm not coming.'

She had stopped him in his tracks. He told her that he had expected some resistance and realised he might have to persuade her, but had not been prepared for such an irrational, stark refusal. He couldn't understand her; he cajoled, he pleaded, he asked for reasons. At first she told him that she had no intention of suddenly asking for time off in a busy period at work, which was something she never did and she was not making an exception.

'OK so work may be a problem, I'll ring Steve and explain. I'm sure he'll understand and agree.'

'You will certainly not ring him. Listen, Tom, you can't just assume. You can't think that I will necessarily fit in with your plans just because you say so.'

He told her that he wasn't assuming, just seeing the chance for them to have a few, wonderful days together. There was a brief silence.

'I hope the conference goes well, Tom, and we'll speak when you return.'

Once she'd rung off and walked into the kitchen, she was wondering quite where all that had come from. Had it been the right decision? Was she just digging her heels in because he had caught her on the hop and she knew she was rather tetchy as it was that time of the month? Was it because she was just a bit miffed to have been taken for granted? Should she ring back? But if she did, what would she say? So many questions when all she had wanted was a cup of tea and an early night. There was no way she would allow herself to drop everything and go, just like that. So, making her tea, she tried to put it out of her mind. That appeared to be no easy matter she found and felt rather bad now this appeared to be their first, significant row.

On Wednesday she got in early and worked really hard, but in her heart of hearts she knew she was doing it partly to justify her decision not to ask for time off, knowing full well her behaviour was irrational, but somehow, she couldn't help herself. When she got home, she wondered whether Tom would ring as he usually did on Wednesday evenings if they weren't meeting up. The house seemed strangely quiet and she felt an unaccustomed restlessness and a need for action. Not knowing how or why she formed the next plan, she decided to go to the tennis club, even though they had previously agreed not to this week, and then call at the late-night supermarket on the way back. Deliberately not thinking through this course of action any further, she nevertheless knew her motives weren't very good ones. If pressed, she understood she was trying to obstruct the possibility of having to answer the phone. She assumed, no she couldn't do that in the light of what she had told him, she expected that Tom would be very angry. When she got home later that evening, there was no message on the answerphone.

It was just after lunch on Thursday when Steve appeared at her office door.

'Need to talk, have you got a few minutes?'

'Sure have.'

He sat down opposite and started to explain that a company called LYonnesse Ltd had rung him to ask if the firm could do a piece of work at very short notice. Gabriella smiled at the same words, "very short notice" cropping up again. Must be the default time-setting for everyone this week, she thought, but listened as Steve continued.

'I've agreed that we'll look at the work involved and see whether we can take it on.'

Gabriella was immediately interested, something new, something different to do.

'What's involved, have you got any details?'

Steve told her that there was an amount of background material to put into order as the information spanned about ten years, research on appropriate legislation to complete, a report to write and copies of an executive summary to prepare.

'I'm getting some further details and the background stuff sent over and we have till five this evening to give them a decision. If we do take it on, it'll mean you and I would have to work long hours, as Mr Solomans, the client, needs the finished work by lunch-time on Saturday.'

'Well you can count me in. As it happens, I would welcome some distraction therapy for the next few days.'

Once she had said that, she had to explain to Steve about Tom's Rome invitation. He was genuinely upset that she had refused to go.

'Of course you could have gone, you silly girl.'

'I know I could have gone, but that wasn't the point.'

Steve slapped his forehead with his hand.

'When I've got about three hours to spare some time, remind me to ask you to explain the workings of the female mind, please.'

She laughed and Steve rose to return to his office and await the arrival of the promised courier.

'I'll give you a call when I've had a preliminary look at what's involved.'

They met at four.

'What do you think? Can we do it in the time? There's no margin for error.'

Gabriella had taken a quick look through the material and read the client's requirement.

'Yes, I think it's doable.'

'Is that an honest opinion?'

She nodded.

'Then we'll tell LYonnesse we'll take it on. Prepare for some serious overtime.'

Once the decision had been made, Gabriella went back to her office, finished one or two tasks, gave some others to Alex, diverted her phone and dealt with a few urgent emails. She grabbed a coffee and then made a start on the research which Steve had given her. She was delighted to have this challenge as she could put Tom completely out of her mind with a good conscience. Because the deadline was going to be very tight, she worked until nearly eight-thirty before wearily making her way out to the car park and heading for home. She was really tired when she got in, but needed some tea, a sandwich and a hot shower to ease a pretty vicious backache. Despite noticing there were two messages on the answer machine, she decided to ignore them. They could be dealt with in the morning.

Tom was not in a good mood when he arrived at the hotel and found the conference suite, barely making it from the airport in time for the start. Following the Chairman's opening remarks, he looked around and waited for the ensuing discussion. Within a few minutes he realised that they were missing the point completely, too insular in their approach, failing to see the bigger picture. Realising that his already pretty bad mood was not going to improve listening to this rubbish, he mentally switched off, put on his professional conference delegate's interested face and started to doodle. He also started to think about Gabriella. He had been such a fool to assume she would just drop everything because he said so and he wondered how much of a fool she thought he was. He was also angry that this wretched conference should be the reason for their falling out. Those words "falling out" had a sinister ring in his mind. Suppose this was a permanent falling out and there was to be no falling back in? He couldn't begin to imagine what he would do if he had lost her because of this stupid trip. He kept seeing wonderful pictures of her in his mind, playing tennis in that short white skirt, standing beside him at his kitchen sink or pushing her sunglasses up onto her head as they wandered through a country lane together. Then he remembered the soft contours of her breasts and the smooth thighs which he was having increasing difficulty with because they just asked to be... He was suddenly aware that the chairman was winding up the session and congratulating them all on the debate it had sparked. He couldn't believe what he was hearing, wished that Vim was about, before realising that he could make good his escape and get back to his room.

Once there he rang room service, threw his jacket on the bed, loosened his tie, settled down in the armchair and glanced at the Agenda for the rest of the day. His heart sank even further and positively plummeted when he read on, seeing that dinner tonight was a formal occasion for all the delegates. Horrors. He wished even more fervently that Vim had been here and they might have hatched a plan together, but as it was, he would have to endure a few hours of boring conversation and try to slide away as quickly as possible. Migraine, which he had never suffered from in his life, seemed a plausible excuse if need be. Oh well, this was what they paid him for, so he had just better get on with it.

Packing up from the afternoon session he heaved a huge sigh, both frustrated at the waste of the last few hours and relieved that Day One was over and took the lift back to his room. Throwing his bedroom window as wide open as it would go, and wondering why hotel rooms always seemed to resemble saunas, he stretched out on the bed and tried to relax. It was still a while before dinner and he wanted, more than anything, to hear Gabriella's voice and to tell her how much he loved her and how sorry he was for getting things so badly wrong. He needed to patch this up as quickly as possible, know things would be OK again and be able to put this behind them. After he had showered and changed, he thought it would be just the right time to ring her, calculating that she would certainly be home from work. It was when the answerphone kicked in that he realised he could only leave a message.

'Gabriella, it's Tom. I just want to say how really, really sorry I am for upsetting you and making you cross. I was stupid and I know that. Please forgive me and ring me back between ten and eleven your time, I so want to talk to you. I love you.'

Disappointed, he went down to the corporate dinner which was every bit as boring as the conference sessions had been and seemed a fitting end to Tom's miserable day. However, the day got worse, because he stayed up until way past one a.m. waiting for his phone to ring. But the phone stayed silent.

Gabriella's alarm shrilled into her consciousness at six a.m. on Friday and she was up, dressed and in the kitchen within twenty minutes. As she drank a quick cup of tea, she listened to her phone messages. The first was a lady telling her she has been specially selected to win a free cruise. That was deleted. The second message was from Tom. Listening, she thought he sounded very apologetic, very down and a long way away and by the end of his message, she realised that she had missed his deadline last night, but that couldn't be helped. She made a mental note to deal with the call later. She was still in no mood to consider what to do about Tom, even an apologetic one. Now it was hit the road and resume work, to have her part ready to hand over when Steve arrived.

The whole of Friday morning was one of intense concentration and constant work until twelve-thirty when she broke for lunch and Steve decided he would come for half an hour as well. At the deli cafe, Gabriella ordered a chicken Caesar salad, Steve a beef sandwich and, settling at a table in a corner, they discussed how they were doing with what had been nicknamed Project Lion. Then, taking another bite of his sandwich, Steve looked at her.

'Talked to Tom, yet?'

Gabriella explained about missing his message on the answerphone.

'You're still a bit cross about what he did, though, aren't you?'

She thought for a moment, hearing the rowdy hissing of the coffee machine and the calls of the staff reciting orders or hailing customers, then shrugged.

'A bit, yes.'

'Want a few thoughts on the matter from a male perspective?'

'Oh rather. You know that's not a specialist subject of mine!'

As they ate, Steve explained that when men were faced with an argument or some sort of upset, their reaction was quite simple: get it sorted, forget it and move on. Women, he believed (from years of experience, he added with a grin,) tended to fret and brood about things much more, even hold grudges and generally draw things out at far greater length.

'When you're angry,' he was waving a knife in her direction, 'you don't explode and then get over it, instead you go on a slow burn, a bit like a long length of white phosphorous fuse. I don't expect Tom will be prepared for that sort of reaction.'

Gabriella looked down at her plate and fiddled her fork through the remains of her salad. She knew that, as usual, her boss was right.

'Thanks, Steve. I'll see him as soon as he comes back. I mean I must talk it through face to face.'

Steve had finished his sandwich and was wiping his face with a serviette.

'Do you know what you're going to say?'

'Sort of,' she replied, putting down her fork with the kind of gesture that closed the conversation.

When Steve had left, Gabriella told herself that she needed both the full hour away from her desk plus a pot of tea and a large slice of cake. When the tea came, she took out her phone and decided that although she was pretty hopeless at texting, hating using abbreviations and even figures instead of proper words, she would compose a short message to Tom. She owed him at least the courtesy of a reply.

'Not home to reply to ur msg last night. Full msg on ur home phone.G.'

Pausing to shop for milk and bread, she made her way back to the office where she settled down at her desk again, calculating that she must finish another project while Steve completed the report and then she would have time to write the executive summary. But she was aware that time was not on their side and they still had some way to go before completion. Well, they would just have to stay at the office until it was done. She was about to crack on when Steve appeared at her door.

'Got an idea to put to you about delivering this stuff.'

He was leaning against the door frame and Gabriella noticed that he looked tired. Needs a holiday she thought.

'You can say yes or no, it's entirely up to you.'

He explained that while they could get the report and the executive summaries couriered to Mr Solomans, he had received a phone call to say that the man himself was at his country retreat for the weekend. When Steve had looked up the address, he had noted that the village was about thirty minutes' drive from Upton Peploe.

'So, as you're the personable face of the firm, if you want to drive out to the country, you could deliver the stuff to the client and at least put a face to a name. But, you may want to call it a day once we've finished here, so, it's your choice as I said. He needs it by lunch-time tomorrow so he can work on it.'

The words "lunch-time" suddenly sparked an idea in Gabriella's mind.

'I'll be happy to take it, but do me a favour, please. Would you ring him and say I'll deliver the stuff about noon, but I'd like him to recommend somewhere in the area for a reasonable lunch?'

'Great. Thanks. I'll tell him your lunch expenses will be on his bill as you're saving him a courier's fee.'

'Er. No. Not necessary. I may not be eating alone...although equally, I suppose I might be.'

Steve looked at her with a slightly amused expression, started to leave and then turned back.

'Remember, it wasn't such a great crime he committed and treat him gently.'

She raised her eyebrows and sort of nodded.

After Steve had gone and because she hadn't got started yet, she thought she had better just give Alex a heads-up on how long it would be before she could pass over the stuff he needed to put together and make sure he knew they were likely to be working late. She found Alex was itching to get on with the presentation side of things as he believed even the most mediocre piece of work looked better if presented in a nice folder or bound rather than stapled.

'Can you stick labels on straight?' he enquired with a stern expression.

She assured him she would try her best, and as she was leaving the general office, Steve shouted that he had the name of a pub for her.

'"The Laughing Pheasant," what a wonderful name, I suppose he was laughing because he hadn't got shot.'

'Yes well, it'll only be poor old Tom in the line of fire this time.'

Steve's face was wreathed in one of his most wicked grins as she walked out of his office with as much dignity as she could muster, knowing that her boss was having a bit of a laugh at her expense.

Still not having got started, and having heard his name, she also remembered that she needed to leave a message on Tom's house phone and, as she took out her mobile, realised how little she had thought about him over the last forty-eight hours. A frisson of apprehension skidded through her because when she got home tonight, that would have to change. She needed to be prepared for Saturday lunch-time.

* * *

The Friday morning conference session was better, as they had a visiting speaker, a Professor Lipi from a nearby University. Tom listened intently, partly because, although he spoke good English, the professor spoke it with quite a heavy accent, and partly because he was putting forward some interesting and novel ideas. Thankfully they had staggered to lunch-time on Day Two and the sooner it would all be over and he could get home, the better. Or would it?

Tom was preparing to doze and doodle through the afternoon session and had just poured himself a tumbler of water when he was aware of a text message. Furtively looking at his phone under his conference table, he realised it was from Gabriella and knew he couldn't stay in the room.

He just had to get out and read it privately. Scribbling a note of apology to the chairman, he passed it to the chap sitting next to him, got up and quickly walked out. He found a quiet (or less noisy) chair next to a huge plant with glossy green leaves in the corner of the entrance lobby and read the short text. He re-read it because he couldn't get his mind round its meaning. How could she have been out all night? Where? Who with? He closed his eyes for a moment and tried to make some sense of what he had read, but nothing made sense except a feeling that he had really blown it and the message on his home phone would probably say something like, "Nice meeting you and goodbye."

He heaved a sigh, something he seemed to have been doing a lot of over the last few days and with nothing else to do, was about to walk back to the conference room when he suddenly realised that if she was using her phone, he could ring her. He grabbed his mobile, thumped back down onto the chair, found the number and punched the call button. When the mechanical voice told him the phone was switched off, he cursed for not thinking about it sooner. But, if her mobile was off and it was afternoon, she would be working, so he could ring the office. He found that number and called it, but this time a mechanical voice told him that if he held, his call would be transferred to another extension. He couldn't believe this; he was engulfed by a wall of silence. How can you be engulfed by a wall? You're losing it Tom Scotford. Having remonstrated angrily with himself, he snapped his phone shut and stomped moodily back into the conference. But "How to Dominate Markets in a Financial Downturn" was the least of his worries.

CHAPTER 8

By eight o'clock they had finished. Alex had done a magnificent job of producing some really classy folders for the executive summaries onto which he had got Gabriella to fix a discreet label bearing the firm's logo. The report was bound and placed in a separate box. They took Project Lion to the car park and loaded it into Gabriella's boot, then hugged each other, all three knowing that they had done an exceptional piece of work in the timescale.

* * *

Tom didn't hear a word of the remainder of the session, all he could focus on was that she had disappeared out of his life and he couldn't do anything about it. He was sitting in this hotel conference room cursing himself again for having let this happen. He tried to find a comforting, rational explanation about not being able to get through to her by phone, but there was none and he was hating every minute of being in Rome. He thought how his life had been so good for the last few weeks; he was in love, properly in love he thought for the first time in his life, and look what a mess he was making of things. The inability to act or influence events was really bugging him. The afternoon chuntered on interminably. But the time passed somehow and at five-thirty and not a moment too soon, the conference was over and the delegates were doing the usual back-slapping routine before leaving. What a stupid time to end, he thought, the traffic will be snarled up by now and the taxi to the airport would take twice as long. With that thought came a sudden, horrific realisation. He wouldn't be leaving, at least not unless he could change his flight. Thinking Gabriella would be with him, he had not booked their return flight until Sunday. When she had said no, he hadn't even bothered to cancel her ticket and had simply told the hotel that Miss

Devonshire was not able to come after all and he would pay the cancellation charges. Berating himself for not remembering till now, he hurried down to the hotel reception desk, awash with delegates checking out and stood, fretting, until he could enlist the help of a suave Italian who seemed to be the most switched-on of the staff he had encountered. Twenty minutes later, to his absolute despair, he was booked on the first available flight out, on Saturday morning. He had to stay in Rome one more night.

'Thank you. Here,' Tom passed the Italian receptionist a high-value Euro note, 'for you.'

The receptionist thanked him and looked absolutely amazed at an Englishman who tipped so generously.

Slowly returning to his room, he did most of his packing, then showered and changed into the clothes he intended to wear for the flight. He lay on his bed for a while, gazing at the ceiling and looking at the ornate moulding of the central ceiling rose. The word reminded him that someone at the club had referred to Gabriella as an English rose and that set him off. He started going over all the places he had been with her, replaying the best bits like a silent film in his mind and wondering if, as he truly believed, memories were all he was going to be left with. He felt absolutely wretched, raw and really very angry with himself.

At around seven he checked back at reception, mercifully quieter now, to find everything arranged for his departure and, deciding the bar was the only place to offer any solace at all, wandered off down the corridor. Walking through it, he noticed a row of shops which he had not previously bothered to look at. One was a rather fine looking jewellers and gazing in the window at some very lovely, modern pieces, realised that he could buy something for Gabriella. He had hardly bought her any presents and he suddenly wanted to very much. If it turned out to be a farewell gift, then he hoped she might keep it and remember him sometimes. Another thought from quite deep down was threatening to surface as he remembered other times and other gifts.

He stepped inside, the floor was deeply carpeted and the atmosphere spoke of quality and luxury. Browsing around the glass cases filled with beautiful items, he noticed a pendant, it was gold but had some sort of stone set in it as well. What attracted him was that the whole thing looked like a teardrop.

'Good evening sir, are you looking for anything in particular?'

An assistant had walked quietly up behind him. Tom wondered yet again how the English were always recognised by foreigners and explained that he just wanted a gift and he would like a closer look at the gold pendant on the top shelf. The young man took it out and gave it to him.

'It is a very nice piece, sir. Gold, as you see.'

Tom nodded.

'But what's the stone?'

'It is a moonstone, sir. Not particularly valuable, the value is in the gold, but the two go together well I think.'

Tom thought so too and said he would buy it. When the purchase was complete, he slipped the small, black box into his jacket pocket and walked slowly into the bar. Simply buying something for Gabriella helped to lift his mood a fraction and it really was a lovely piece of jewellery. He thought that the teardrop shape was particularly appropriate and he would give it to a beautiful young lady who never asked for anything from him. How she would receive it was another matter. That other thought was threatening to rise again from a deeper place in his memory, but he forced it back down, got to the bar and ordered a double gin and tonic.

At eight o'clock he went into the restaurant, found a quiet table and ate a reasonable seafood pasta dish accompanied by a couple of glasses of Pinot Grigio wine. Thankfully the restaurant was reasonably quiet and not very full as it was too early, he suspected, for many diners. He started to think back over the last month or so. It had all been going well, he thought, until now. What a mess you've made. Will there be a second chance? He drank his coffee deep in thought. He was supposed to be good at things, some people called him a high-flier. Well he wasn't feeling very expert at the moment and he was near rock bottom in terms of emotional confidence and had no idea how this was going to end. He sat for a while, but then roused himself into action and started to formulate a plan for the evening, a very different evening from the one he had imagined. He paid his bill and walked back to reception, asking for a tourist map and receiving some general directions, together with a few astonished looks when he told the desk staff what he was proposing. Then, standing on the hotel steps, he tried to orientate himself because he was going to walk down to the River Tiber. He knew it was quite a long way, miles in fact even if he didn't get lost, but he thought he could do it and he set off.

After about half an hour's steady walk he saw a street sign, located it on his map and was pleased he was still heading in the right direction. Walking through one of the most beautiful cities in the world he was seeing virtually nothing around him, the elegant buildings and the plaster work and wrought iron generally escaped his notice as he pressed on. Even though he knew his hotel was not far from the famous Trevi Fountain, he was in no mood for sightseeing. What was supposed to happen there? If you threw in a coin, it would ensure your return to Rome. Well, he couldn't wait to leave the city and certainly had no plans to return. Ambling slowly through the streets and narrow alleyways, he frequently had to sidestep young couples who were entwined in a passionate embrace in the middle of the pavement, oblivious to all but themselves. It was another reminder of how he had planned a similar night and how his plans had been thrown out, bathwater and baby. Whenever he came to an open space where there were seats, he sat down for short rests and, in this leisurely way it took him nearly two hours to reach the banks of the Tiber. Although he had seen little around him, he was aware of how many people were still out and about. Traffic was spewing from every side street into main roads which were clogged to a crawling pace. There were only a few tranquil corners; mostly the air vibrated with noise, as on such a warm night in summer, Rome - like any large city - hardy seemed to sleep. He had passed bars and cafes and it would have been easy to let the night life of the city swallow him up, but he was not in the mood. He was going to walk to the river, it seemed a solitary enough thing to do to fill the hours of the night and he was quite content with that.

He found a bridge with a steep flight of steps down to the riverside and looked at the water flowing past like a huge, black silky ribbon, with both beauty and menace in its dark depths. Its darkness exactly matched his mood he thought and in that dark mood, all he could think about was Gabriella. He desperately wanted to be back to pick up her message, but he was truly afraid of what the outcome might be. He looked at his watch, it was getting late he thought and then realised that it was in fact nearly early morning, he ought to think about finding a return route. He didn't want to re-trace his steps, but believed he would go back to a footbridge he had passed and that would allow him to find a return route to his hotel. If all else failed, he trusted there would be taxis still out looking for custom. He eventually found the bridge, left the riverbank and started back towards his hotel, at least that's what he hoped he was doing. He walked on, quite slowly, feeling more emotionally than physically weary, but anyway, there was no hurry, he had nothing else to do. The traffic had calmed down and the night was less noisy around him. He was deep in thought and didn't realise that a black car had drawn up alongside and stopped in front of him. The window slid noiselessly down.

'You should not walk here, it is not safe.'

The driver was a dark-haired beauty about his own age or perhaps a bit older.

'Get in, I will take you.'

He was momentarily disorientated, she was beautifully made up, and she was smiling at him and indicating the passenger seat of the car. Because he was alone, because he had walked a huge distance, because her voice had jolted him out of deep thoughts, he looked at her and wondered where he was and what was happening. Good looking, dark hair, smart clothes, immaculate make up, he thought it was Caroline who had somehow managed to find him in Rome. Those were the memories which he had been suppressing all evening. Then he remembered where he was, and that this lady was Italian.

'No, grazie,' he managed to summon up a few words.

'Grazie, I er I walk.'

She looked at him for a long, cool moment and as he stepped back away from the kerb, gave a little shrug.

'Arrivederci.'

The window slid up, the car pulled away and, still slightly disorientated, he watched the rear lights disappear before setting off again towards the hotel. Those memories now were dancing in the forefront of his mind with tremendous force. A powerful force, just like Caroline. Buying the gift for Gabriella, who had never, ever asked him for anything, who wouldn't even countenance expensive gifts, had rekindled the memories of the woman who expected anything and everything and then the dark-haired beauty had added fuel to his tired brain.

The night staff didn't seem at all surprised to see him enter the lobby at two-thirty and once in his room he stretched out, trying to doze while he waited for his early call, but Caroline was refusing to go away. Lying on his hotel bed, he remembered their love-making and he wondered how and when he would first make love with Gabriella. He knew that would be something really special, and could hardly bear the intense feelings the thought provoked as he imagined their bodies coming together in pure love and perfect harmony and then the fireworks exploding. It would be perfection. A cooler breeze drifted in through the open window and he wanted to get home to the beautiful English girl who might or might not still be there for him.

When his plane taxied from its stand at Fiumicino Airport just after eight-thirty on Saturday morning, he sat in his seat, watching the tarmac race beneath them and thought about what he needed to do. As the plane rose into the air and the tarmac was replaced first by bulbous, white clouds, then wispy greyness, he began to collect his thoughts and plan for his return. Yes, it had been a pretty dire couple of days, but if this had been back at work where something had gone wrong, he knew he would be busting a gut by now to retrieve the situation. OK he had tried and been thwarted and he still didn't know why he had been unable to make any contact with Gabriella. But he had to regard that as a temporary setback. Now, get home and sort this out.

* * *

On Saturday, the lie-in until eight-thirty was a welcome luxury after the previous two early starts and Gabriella was pleased that life had slowed at last. After a bowl of cereal and a mug of tea, she showered before opening the wardrobe doors to select suitable clothes, wanting something that would look reasonably businesslike, though not too formal to wear for the pub. The thought of the pub made her think of Tom. Last night she had spent some time getting her thoughts in order. They really had to talk this incident through as she was pretty sure he hadn't any idea why she had been so focused in her refusal.

None of her clothes seemed to be exactly what she wanted. She picked out a long, floral skirt, held it against her and then put it back. Too informal. She needed to explain a few things, notably like not assuming stuff would happen and not expecting everyone to fall in with his plans. Ah, the new linen dress was a possibility and she swung it off the rail. But Tom had seen that and for some obscure reason, she wanted to be dressed in something different. So that went back. Anyway, she didn't even know whether he had got her message giving him directions to join her for lunch, but if he did turn up, at least she was sure of the things she wanted to say. She slipped a short-sleeved navy dress, which she had bought last year and not worn much, off its hanger, held it against her body and thought it looked OK. She had navy wedge heeled sandals and could take a white linen jacket if necessary. Yes. She slipped it on over her head and surveyed her image. For once, she bothered to put her hair up, securing it at the back with a comb and then re-checked her reflection in the mirror.

'Mmm, not bad.'

Mr Solomans didn't look anything like the gentleman she had imagined. He was tall and portly with an astounding mass of grey, wire wool hair which fell almost to his shirt collar and had a fleshy red nose, a mouth with full lips and teeth which revealed a large gap between the front two when he smiled. He was, however, extremely pleasant and jovial and delighted to see her with the work he had commissioned.

'I have to say, this looks extremely well put together,' he remarked, eyeing the executive summary folders. 'Please convey my thanks to Steve and all who have helped. I shall be rather occupied for the next three days or so, but I will ring him as soon as I am able.'

Gabriella told him that the firm had been glad to help.

'And now, I shall go to see what "The Laughing Pheasant" has to offer.'

'I do hope it meets your expectations, I think it will and thank you again,' he said as he retreated into his house with his report and summaries. He turned and waved before closing the door and he sort of reminded her of a character in a film or possibly on TV but she couldn't quite place who it was.

Driving out of the village, turning at the next junction in the direction of Middleton Magna, Gabriella found the pub at one end of the main village street and parked in an almost empty car park. As she had time to spare, she decided mentally to rehearse the points she needed to get over to Tom. So, sitting in her car, eyes not really focusing on her surroundings, she tried to visualise the scene where she would be in control of discussions and she hoped they would come to a sound agreement on the way ahead. Put like that, it all sounded relatively simple, but she was still rehearsing some of the points and hoping she was fully prepared for any battle which might lie ahead as she pushed open the door.

The pub was old with low beams and huge stone fireplaces, unlit now in the summer but promising welcome warmth come winter time. The decor of cream and dark yellow gave it a light and spacious feel which counteracted the lowness of the ceilings and the small, leaded windows. There were pictures of pheasants on all the walls and a rather fierce looking stuffed one in a glass case under the sign for the toilets. It looked quite an amusing place, and she could easily see the jovial Mr Solomans making this his local. She wandered into the restaurant and told the waiter she had booked a table. Being offered a choice of two, she selected one where Tom could easily see her when he came in, assuming he had got her message, assuming he had decided to come. Oh that damned word again! Now that she had got to this point, she was not sure whether she wanted to see him or not. Yes, of course she did. It was just that she knew how well life had been going recently and in her experience, that meant it was probably, inevitably, due to go downhill again. She sighed, gazing at the fierce, stuffed bird and wondered if this journey was going to come to a bit of an abrupt end. A bit like his had done she thought. She supposed that Tom had been having a pretty good time in Rome and he might not be in the mood for the things she wanted to say, the things he needed to hear.

The waiter was hovering so she told him she was expecting a friend, ordered an orange juice and a bottle of sparkling water, which was brought, along with a little dish of olives and settled down to look at the menu and wait. She had read both the menu and the specials board and was sitting quietly sipping her drink when she was aware that Tom was almost at the table.

'Tom, you have made it.'

Her heart gave a little jump and she realised that yes, it was nice to see him again.

'Sit down. Let's get you a drink.'

He sat opposite her and she thought there was something different about him, but couldn't put her finger on what it was. She couldn't have forgotten what he looked like in five days. The waiter arrived, Tom asked for an apple juice and Gabriella said that it would be ten minutes or so before they would like to order food.

'No problem, ma'am.'

Tom looked at her, absorbing this information but saying nothing. She was about to ask whether he had found the place easily when the waiter returned with the apple juice. Tom took a sip or two of his drink.

'Well I see that I'm here for the disciplinary interview.'

His tone was flat and steely.

'The what?'

She was startled by his words and the tone in his voice.

'You know, at work, when you've done something wrong, you get summoned to an interview. I think it's going to be like that because,' he glanced round at the room, 'we appear to be on neutral ground and you're not quite dressed as I would imagine for Sunday lunch in a country pub.'

She was about to launch into the speech she had prepared, but before she could speak, he went on.

'I know I got things badly wrong. I assumed that what I wanted to happen would be OK but I had no right to do that. I'm truly sorry, it won't happen again.'

To say she was taken aback was putting it mildly, it wasn't his turn to speak, according to the way she had planned their talk, but Tom didn't seem to have read the script.

'Yes, but it did happen and I'm not sure why you expected it would be alright.'

She thought she had managed to get started on her side of the argument, but before she could draw breath, he was speaking fast but with great forcefulness.

'I did it because I'm still learning. We haven't been together long, I don't know what to do at times, how to act, I just got it wrong, that's all.'

The torrent continued, forcing her to listen because she could do nothing else.

'I understand now how dedicated you are to your job and that's fine, I think that's a wonderful characteristic and I will learn from this mistake, that's all it was, a simple mistake because I just saw it as a fabulous opportunity to be with you.'

He drew breath and took a long gulp of his drink. She seized the moment.

'Yes, well, it came over as thoughtless assumption on your part and wanting just to do things your way, but I accept what you've said by way of explanation.'

She thought she had wrested back the initiative, but he looked up and fixed her with those blue eyes.

'Gabriella, I may have got this wrong, but I'm not going to lose you, I'm not going to let this spoil what we've achieved so far together. I'll fight to keep you, you need to know that and it doesn't matter where you were or who you were with on Friday night.'

He stopped, looked down at the table and fiddled with the menu. Gabriella was still taken aback. She had expected to be calling the tune but he had come ready to fight his own corner. Her anger was about to rise when she heard Steve's voice somewhere in the back of her brain and realised what was happening. Steve had told her that men liked to get things sorted, and that was just what he was doing. As she looked at him sitting opposite her she also realised what was different about him, he looked absolutely shattered. She took several deep breaths. Don't let your anger burn, she told herself, it was just a mistake, no big deal. She glanced, involuntarily, at the pheasant again, its beady glare seemed to be reproving, admonishing her even. Gradually her anger evaporated and she forgot the prepared speech, which wasn't that important anyway. She had heard his words, "I'll fight to keep you," and she instinctively knew that's what she wanted.

'Tom,' she said gently, 'it's not a disciplinary interview, just let me explain a few things which might help.'

As she started to speak more gently, she noticed that his expression had changed and he was now looking less forceful and more anxious. That subtle shift, together with the pale tiredness in his face, made him look quite unlike the Tom she normally saw. She was also beginning to make sense of his peculiar comments about where she might have been and to see how her strange working pattern over the last few days had caused an added problem.

'Let me explain what I've been doing and with whom.'

She told him about Project Lion, the hours which she and Steve had worked to accomplish it and the delivery she had just made to Mr Solomans' cottage in the next village. She saw a strange expression pass over his face as though things were beginning to make sense at last and he was beginning to understand.

'As I had to come over here, I thought we might be able to meet up and try to work out what went wrong between us.'

He looked at her for a long moment as though he was processing, quite slowly, what she had just said.

'You've been working? Is that why I couldn't contact you at all by phone and you weren't in on Friday?'

'Yes, Steve and I have been working really long days and when I got home late on Friday, I was too tired even to listen to my messages, so I'm sorry I missed the one you left.' He slumped in his chair.

'I thought you were out all night with someone else.'

She looked at him in amazement.

'No. That would've been pretty quick work, you only left on Thursday.'

He managed a weak smile but then looked hard at her again.

'But this invitation to lunch is so we can talk. That's what we're here for isn't it? I was so stupid to take over and assume I could run your life and you would just drop everything because I said so.'

His words were tumbling out again.

'I'm so, so sorry and the conference was dreadful and all the while I kept thinking how awful it was that something so dreadful as that lousy conference had made this happen.'

He looked up and she could see real determination and purpose in his face.

'Gabriella, I'm really not going to lose you, I love you so much and this has only made me realise just how much you mean to me.'

He stopped talking, sat very still and held her gaze intently. She was aware that he just didn't know how those blue eyes could melt her heart. She reached across and took his hand.

'Tom, Tom it's alright, you're not going to lose me.'

'Do you mean that?'

'I mean that. We just need to learn the lessons from this incident, draw a line under it and move on.'

He was gripping her hand fiercely. She explained that he was right in thinking that she had been cross about the way he had assumed he could include her in his plans, however well-meaning, without asking first.

'I know, I know, it was so stupid, I couldn't believe I had done it and I'll never do it again. I've learnt that lesson the hard way, you don't have anything to learn, it was all my fault.' She managed to get him to lessen his grip slightly and then told him how Steve had pointed out something to her about the way she allowed her anger to burn slowly and unnecessarily instead of dealing with it in a better way.

'That's the lesson I need to learn.'

They talked a little more and then agreed that they each had learnt lessons, a line had been drawn and they would move on. Then, as they both thought the food on offer looked really good, and Gabriella was pleased that Tom seemed ready to relax, they decided that food would be good for them both.

'Tom, I never thought I would say this to you, but you look awful!'

He smiled.

'I feel pretty dreadful, but I shall revive now that we've got things straightened out.'

'Tell me about Rome then and why it was so dire and why you look so shattered.'

He explained about the conference and the delegates and how, as she had suspected, he had thought the worst when he was unable to contact her.

'So last night, I walked to the river; it took hours and then it was too late to go to bed because I had changed my flight to the first one this morning.'

'You haven't slept. You walked for most of the night?'

'Yes, there didn't seem anything better to do. But apart from looking at the river, I couldn't tell you where I went or what landmarks I passed, which was a bit of a waste.'

He didn't mention the dark- haired Italian beauty in the car, because he had simply forgotten all about her and the memory she had awakened.

Their meal was excellent and by the time he had eaten, Tom had revived. He told Gabriella that he had only just got home in time to hear her message and come to the pub.

'But I don't care, it's been worth it. I can always catch up on sleep tonight.'

They had coffee and she settled the bill. Tom watched her, this was an independent, professional lady whose life he had entered, almost unasked, and he needed to remember to tread carefully.

'Are you too tired for a short walk? I'd rather like to look at the village now I'm here.'

They walked, hand in hand up the street until they came to a signpost "To the River."

'Shall we go? You can compare it with the mighty Tiber,' she giggled, and, feeling her spirits now quite restored, slipped her hand round his waist. The river was a small chalk-stream, absolutely gin-clear and Gabriella, bending over and trying to see into the depths of the water, was rewarded by the sight of some beautiful trout finning lazily through the weeds. She turned and looked at him. He was standing a little way away from her and she wondered if he was still a bit unsure of quite where they were in their relationship. She walked over to him, reached up and clasped her hands round his neck.

'Are you OK? Steve will want to know if I treated you gently or not.'

He laughed.

'Yes, I'm OK. Tired, but happy.'

Standing so close she could feel both the warmth and the strength of his body and knowing she really wanted to do it, pulled him gently towards her, pressing her body more closely against his. Instantaneously she felt him shudder and then join her in a long, long, kiss which reminded her of their very first one as the rippling, pulsating passion ripped through them both as they stood on the riverbank. It was the most wonderful making-up moment. When she released him and stood back, both seemed to realise that all the perceived anguish of the past few days had been worth it if they could come back together like this. He looked at her.

'Oh, I nearly forgot, I've got a present for you.'

'For me?'

He put a hand into his jacket pocket and brought out the small, black box.

'Yes. I hope you like it. I bought it because it seemed appropriate.'

For once she didn't remonstrate, but simply took the little black box and opened it.

'Tom,' her voice was choked and soft, 'it's so lovely, it looks like a teardrop.'

'I know. That's why I bought it.'

Gazing up at him, she took it out and fastened it round her neck.

'How does it look?'

'Nearly as beautiful as the girl who's wearing it.'

She drew his face down to hers and kissed him gently.

'Darling Tom, thank you. You're so good and kind to me. Please, please don't let's fall out ever again.'

She gazed up at him, seeing his tiredness, mixed with relief and he did look absolutely shattered. They kissed again, slowly this time and he wrapped his arms round her as they stood silently, looking at an English river.

Game, Set and Love Match

CHAPTER 9

After the trauma and then delight of Saturday, they spent most of Sunday together, doing very little, reading the papers and then having a meal in Tom's kitchen. But after the meal, when they had both stretched out on the large sofa and started to kiss, she had realised that the intensity of feeling was building and building and she knew that she didn't want to stop it. He slid her blouse off and dropped the straps of her bra, then when she had felt his hand under her breast she had also felt herself happily responding to his touch. It was that wonderful melting, floating feeling and she was beginning to realise what it was to be loved, desired, by this man. And she was also well aware that with his pure, physical strength, if he wanted to undress her completely, she would be powerless to stop him. But, after the first minutes of passion which threatened to run away with them, he kissed her more gently, laid her back across his lap and looked at her.

'Are you really OK Gabriella? This journey of ours - how do you feel about it?'

She knew he was really asking for reassurance and she also knew what he wanted to hear. But despite the fact that she was responding more and more to him, she had to acknowledge that she was still not as passionately in love with him as he was with her. Taking a deep breath, she decided he needed as honest an answer as she could give.

'I hope you can tell that I am falling in love with you Tom. You're a fabulous person to know and you've been really kind and understanding with the way I want things to go.'

'What, slowly, you mean?'

But he was laughing as he said it, not being critical of her cautiousness.

'Yes, I'm an old slow coach, especially in comparison with you and I do know that you want us to be lovers, that's very clear, but I'm not ready yet. Sorry, my darling. That's how it is, and you did ask.'

'I know. But as long as you're happy and we're still moving forward, even if it's only a centimetre at a time, I'm happy too. But, I'll tell you something that keeps me going.' Kissing her and running his hands round the curves of her waist and hips, he told her that in Rome he had imagined them making love, and when it happened, it would be fabulous. It would be perfect. She looked at him, nodded slightly and twisted her fingers through his. She was beginning to believe it. She was truly beginning to fall in love with this rather special man who had suddenly burst into her life, and that was new and rather scary. But, he'd always told her it would be fabulous and he just might be right.

Sitting at her desk on Monday morning, drinking the first coffee of the day and going over that Sunday conversation in her mind, she didn't hear Steve's arrival.

'Well?'

She jumped, saw her boss standing in the doorway and was in such a good mood, she decided to string him along a bit – for once.

'Very well thank you.'

A little verbal jousting to start with.

'How was Mr Solomans and how was lunch?'

'Mr Solomans was very well also and,' she could see Steve approaching her desk, looking for something to throw, 'he thought the work looked excellent and he wishes everyone to be thanked for their efforts. He'll ring you in about three days.'

'And lunch?'

'Excellent food. Please tell him that it was a very good recommendation.'

'Stop prevaricating, woman. Did he turn up?'

She laughed and gave Steve an account of her lunch with a totally shattered Tom.

'Poor chap, fancy walking half the night, you really seem to have a pretty bad effect on him, I wonder he can put up with you!'

It was her turn to look for something and she threw a packet of Post It notes at him.

'Did you kiss and make up?'

Gabriella hesitated for a moment.

'Yes, we did, eventually. I wasn't quite sure at first how things would work out because he rather got me on the back foot by coming out fighting. I sort of started to get angry again but then I heard your voice telling me that men just like to get things sorted and I guessed that was what he was doing.'

'Excellent, I'm glad my words of wisdom aren't entirely wasted on you,' and he retreated before any heavier missile came his way.

And so, having got through the trauma of Romegate, they had set off again and as both seemed to renew their efforts to please, had a couple of really good weeks. They had gone for a day out to Stratford, done the tourist things and seen a play and been invited to a barbecue at Steve's. This had initially caused Gabriella some anguish as she realised that for the first time, she would be taking Tom with her as a boyfriend. But her colleagues all knew he existed and, she also knew, were dying to meet him. They had had a really great time. As she might have known, Tom charmed everyone and was a huge hit with Steve's two young sons, going off to see their toys and organising an impromptu game of three-a-side football with them. And although Tani and Fay both had young men with them, they had kept sidling up to her whispering, "He's gorgeous." "Pass him over if you like." "Where did you find him?"

Steve had allowed himself a day off on the following Monday, so when he appeared at her office door mid-morning on Tuesday, Gabriella was expecting some comment about Tom.

'Message from Julie, endorsed by me I might add.'

He was looking quite serious and Gabriella wondered exactly what was coming next.

'If you can't make your mind up about this one, then you're a bit of a fool and we don't think you are. So mind you don't lose him, because there aren't too many like him hanging around.'

He suddenly grinned.

'None of our business, we know, but he's a really good chap by the looks of things. Remember, you heard it here first, just in case you were in any doubt!'

He disappeared and Gabriella sat, smiling. Yes, it had been odd the way it had worked out –while not remotely thinking of Tom initially as "Mr Right", he seemed to be just that. But although realising there was a lot of truth in what they were telling her, she also knew that like a dog, a partner should be for life, not just Christmas.

Tom was very busy at work all week and Gabriella didn't bother to go down to the club until Friday. Walking in, she was immediately accosted by Mike.

'Gabriella, you've met our son Kris, haven't you?'

Mike was wearing his proud father expression as Gabriella again looked up into the face of a tall, loose-limbed teenager.

'I certainly have. We played together a few weeks ago – and won.'

'Yeah. I remember, we beat George and that fat woman.'

'Kris.'

His father was now looking less proud.

'Sorry.'

He turned to Gabriella.

'You're good, anyway, so I want to play with you again.'

'That's fine by me, Kris. I gather you've been hard at it with exams. How did they go?'

'Dunno yet, but I think OK.'

He was jiggling about on the spot as only the hyperactive young can, so Gabriella suggested they went out for a bit of a practice and Kris shot off to get balls telling his Dad to get Mum and come out later. Soon after they had started, Gabriella remembered that this teenager was, in fact, a talented player and probably had the potential to be very good.

'You're the good one,' she shouted across at him after he had steered a backhand cross-court well out of her reach.

'Yeah, well, I want to get like Tom and beat him. Have you played against him yet?' He smashed a forehand past her.

'He's awesome.'

Gabriella smiled at yet another member of the Scotford fan club turning up. But she also realised that she and Tom had never played in any foursome together, part of the ploy to keep things secret.

'No, I seem to have missed that pleasure.'

Then a thought struck her.

'Has he given you any coaching?'

'You bet.'

Kris was now practising volleys as she hit a succession of balls to him.

'And one day I'm going to thrash him and have a car like his.'

Gabriella retrieved a couple of balls from near the net. She decided to have a little fun.

'What a silver one you mean?'

Kris snorted in derision.

'You do know what it is, don't you?'

'Haven't the faintest.'

That was sort of true, but she was also winding Kris up gently. She was rewarded by a withering look from her young opponent and a heavy sigh of incomprehension.

'It's only a Quattroporte Sport.'

'Very nice.'

Gabriella was enjoying herself and not worrying unduly that she was engaging in a bit of subterfuge at Kris's expense. But before she could get any further with her lesson on foreign-sounding cars, she saw Mike and Su coming towards them.

'I'm going to play with Gabriella,' Kris shouted as soon as they were within earshot, 'even though she hasn't a clue about decent cars.'

Mike wanted to know what that was all about and Kris explained Gabriella's total lack of appreciation of Tom's car.

'Ah,' Mike was grinning broadly at her, 'you'll find, my son, that Tom has failed to impress Gabriella, so do your best to get into her good books.'

Gabriella, hugely amused but not daring to show it, was about to protest that his comments weren't totally accurate, but Kris was manically bouncing balls and telling them he was ready for some action. It turned out to be one of the best games she had played and they beat

Mike and Su fairly easily in the end. As they walked off court Kris loped along beside her.

'I shall ask for you as a partner anytime I can't play with Tom. That was great, especially as we wupped the old folks.'

Gabriella had to giggle, she liked Kris. He was completely natural, what you saw was what you got and he had a real effervescent quality about him as well as a scathing wit. She also knew that he would be disappointed if he was hoping to play with Tom, because he was working late this particular Friday evening, more was the pity for both her young friend and herself, she thought.

Cadmore High Street was busy on Saturdays and Gabriella checked the time as she walked from the hairdressers. An hour in the Beauty Parlour and a shorter, layered haircut had made her feel like a new woman. Hope Tom likes it she thought, a bit anxious now that she had done the deed. Retrieving her car from the multi-storey, she drove back home. It was mid-afternoon and she didn't want to do much before she changed and went out, so as this was an unaccustomed pampering day, she curled up with the weekend paper and a magazine. Rarely allowing herself this sort of day and still feeling a bit guilty about spending money and time just being beautified, she also loaded the washing machine ready to put it on for an overnight wash when she got back later. That salved her conscience a little, but as she had put her tennis skirt in the wash, she would have to decide whether to wear the very old one or the very new one. She had not had the courage to wear the second of the new ones she had bought yet, but it was really, really nice. Climbing the stairs, she took the skirt out of the wardrobe. It had a gored hem and was designed to swish out when the wearer moved. She'd seen a girl in a televised tournament wearing a similar one and feared that folks might think it was too professional-looking for Upton Peploe. Oh stop beating yourself up so, you bought it, you liked it, put it on. Once dressed, she knew exactly why she had liked it and suddenly felt alright about both her new hair and her new skirt. Perhaps there will be new tennis balls tonight she mused. It was a bit of a club joke that George was notoriously parsimonious when it came to the provision of new balls and people only laughed at his protestations of how expensive they were.

Parking up, she got her bag and walked towards the pavilion. Waving to Mike and Su, she plopped her bag onto a bench in the empty room and went out to sit with them.

'Who's this new girl then?'

Mike was looking at her.

'That looks lovely, when did you have it done?' Su enquired, giving her husband a slight kick in the ankle.

She recounted her visit to Anton's and was pleased that so far, her new look was getting a good reaction. Shading her eyes with a hand she looked at the two players.

'Kris will be pleased to be getting a game of singles, he said he would get Tom to come early, so I see he has.'

The three spectators watched in companionable silence for a while.

'Gosh.'

Gabriella couldn't help herself. She had been watching Tom closely, something she had rarely been able to do and noticed again just how tall, elegant and athletic he actually was.

'I didn't realise Tom was quite that good, I've never seen him play this well.'

Su smiled.

'Yes, I don't think Kris is going to beat him tonight, but he'll be enjoying the challenge anyway. Tom seems in a very good mood these days, much more light-hearted than he was a while ago. Don't you think so?'

She had turned to her husband.

'Oh, goodness, I don't keep track of his every mood and gesture like you lot do, he just seemed normal to me.'

Gabriella smiled but said nothing.

Within five minutes several other cars had arrived and the three of them rose and made their way towards the pavilion. As they passed the court entrance Tom shouted to Mike.

'We're just going to finish now that others have come, so we'll be in after this game.'

George and Alice were inside talking to three others, one of whom Gabriella hardly knew and two who were complete strangers, probably visitors. Introductions were made and she tried to commit the new names to memory. When George had finished sorting people out, Gabriella wasn't surprised that he had got himself playing in a four with Tom (she had noticed how he normally wangled that) but amazed that she was in it as well, together with the lady she hardy knew. The others who were playing had already left the pavilion, Kris pulling a rather mournful face she noted.

'Do you know this is the first time I've played in a foursome with or against you?'

Tom looked at her, and a slow smile spread across his face.

'Which is it to be then, partners or opposition?'

Although it was a choice, she knew he was really offering her a challenge.

'Oh, it's got to be opposition, hasn't it? I mean I have to test myself against the best. And,' she rounded on him, 'I shall be playing to win.'

He just grinned at her and walked to the other side of the court. When he got there, he looked back,

'And so shall I, Miss Devonshire.'

Partnering George, she knew they would be a reasonably strong couple, but she had no idea what Anne, who was to play with Tom, was like. Once they started to play she soon realised they were pretty equally matched. Anne was an average sort of player, but Tom could cover so much of the court, it didn't make much difference what she was like. They got to two-one and it was Gabriella's service next. Tom picked up the spare balls and brought them to the net to hand to her.

'Well,' his eyes were shining with merriment, 'crunch time on your service, Gabriella.'

She noticed that Anne had also come to the net and was drinking from a water bottle, so in the pause, she looked at him, enjoying the renewed moment of challenge.

'Yes, so I'll need some good serves, aces in fact. So what's your best advice, Mr Scotford?'

They were both enjoying this.

'You know how to serve aces. Think technique, power and placement. Easy.'

He turned away, then, looked at her over his shoulder.

'Just believe you're good enough.'

Walking back and holding the balls she was going to serve, Gabriella had never felt so competitive in her life. She remembered what he had told her, because she had to win both points when serving to Anne if they were to stand a chance. She breathed deeply, tossed a ball high, reached up and brought her racket to it at the highest point. It was past Anne before she had moved. Excellent. So far, so good. Now, the difficult bit. She couldn't replicate the ace and Tom drilled a return at George who put a difficult volley into the net.

'Hey, steady on, Tom. That nearly went through me.'

'Sorry, George, it was a good service, made me keep the ball low.'

Scores level. Must win the next point. Out of the corner of her eye she saw Tom telling Anne to stand a little further to her right. So, she thought, he doesn't think I can hit one down the centre line, but I believe I can. Gabriella hit the ball as hard as she could, it flew over the net, close to the centre line, but it was out. Damn. Ready with another ball, she regrouped. She had a strategy. Tossing the ball up, she took some of the pace off, but hit it down the centre again and in. Anne was expecting a change of direction and could only lunge, belatedly, as the ball sped past her flailing racket. They had to get the next point and she was sure that Tom would target her instead of George to try to win it. The serve was as good as she could hope for, but, as she had expected, the ball came screaming back across the net towards her. Having anticipated it though, she got a racket on it and hit it back, steering it away from Tom. Anne managed to return the ball and it was almost like watching in slow motion as George lunged across the court in front of her and hit a winner. She knew they could win the last point and they did.

'Game, two all.' George boomed sonorously as Gabriella punched the air with an exultant whoop. However, although putting up a huge fight, she and George eventually lost, but Gabriella couldn't have cared less.

Stepping into the pavilion after having stopped for a word with the players on the other court, Gabriella came face to face with Tom, who appeared to have been waiting for her arrival.

'Well young lady,' he put a hand briefly on her shoulder, 'you served that game out fantastically well.'

He was grinning mischievously.

'Well done, I think you play better in that skirt.'

She laughed back into his face.

'Or perhaps I can run faster with less hair.'

Fortunately, Tom was not forced into any public comment on her appearance as they were interrupted by George's booming tones, asking if any people wanted to play on as he and Alice had to go. Most of the others decided on at least another few games and Gabriella managed to get into a foursome to partner Kris who was still whingeing about the game he had just played in with two visitors. Gabriella had to hush him as he was making his feelings terribly and rather loudly known. Eventually, although it was a bit early to finish, most players were ready to go for a drink, except Kris who pleaded for some more singles with Tom.

'Oh, alright, but only fifteen minutes, as I have to buy Gabriella a drink for her outstanding serving tonight.'

They disappeared, Kris now muttering to Tom about the absolutely useless game that he'd previously played in and Mike and Gabriella grinning as they listened.

'Where's Su.?'

'Already gone up for a drink I suspect. Coming?'

'Just going to the car, then I will.'

Mike walked with her to the car.

'How're your knees, then?'

Gabriella, having thrown her bag into the boot, straightened up, looked at him and then down at her legs.

'Fine, why?'

He looked at her with a wicked little grin.

'Oh I thought back in the pavilion they just might be buckling a bit, that's all.'

She stood still and burst out laughing, then locked her car and they started back. She could use this for a bit of deflection strategy.

'Oh, Tom you mean. Ah, I think he's on a bit of a charm offensive because I told him I was not too impressed with him on first acquaintance.'

'You didn't?'

Mike was laughing now.

'I surely did. And I told him what all the women say about him.'

Mike looked at her incredulously.

'Hell's bells, what did he say? Did you tell him he was the local sex symbol?'

'Not exactly in those words, I didn't.'

'But how did he react?'

She thought back to the conversation, remembering to be suitably guarded in what she said.

'At first I think he was genuinely amazed and a bit embarrassed because I honestly don't think he's vain about his looks and I gathered he had no idea of the effect he can have on some members of the opposite sex. Then he found it very funny.'

'Yeah, that's what I would've expected. I guess it would have come as something of a shock.'

Gabriella suddenly thought she needed to get off this topic of conversation.

'Now, not another word, and don't tell the other ladies he knows,' she pleaded, 'or they'll stop talking about him and that would ruin my fun.'

* * *

On Monday morning Tom was sitting at his desk indulging in a few moments' reflection, moulding a pile of paper clips on a magnetic base into what he intended to be The Angel of The North. Then it drooped pathetically and fell over. The last few weeks had been, well, a steep learning curve would be one description, marvellously exciting and frustratingly slow-moving the other. But he was beginning to feel they were closer and he was daring to hope that Gabriella was starting not only to trust him but her own instincts as well. He smiled ruefully. She couldn't possibly know how hard he was having to hold back at times and how he ached to make love to her, to claim her and know that she wanted him wholeheartedly, unconditionally. Well, he thought, a little abstinence won't hurt you. But he closed his eyes and let the images of them together which had swirled around his mind in Rome envelop him for a brief moment. Then, flattening the remains of The Angel, he started work.

They spoke on the phone most evenings and on Tuesday Tom detected a flatter note in her voice and asked whether there was anything the matter. He heard a little sigh at the other end of the phone and a pause, which usually meant she was marshalling her thoughts as he had found she always tried to find the right words to express what she was thinking. Or it could mean she was hesitating about telling him something.

'Oh, it's nothing really. I'm getting a bit anxious about Steve going on holiday and having to run the office and...'

'But you'll be fine,' he interjected, immediately recognising her worry-syndrome.

'You're conscientious and I believe from what you've said that you like your job and you must be good at it as well.'

'How do you work that out, from absolutely no knowledge?'

He could only hear a slightly querulous tone in her voice as she asked it and knew he was in for another patient explanation session.

'Because if Steve didn't think you were competent, he'd simply close the office for a fortnight and send everyone on holiday at the same time.'

'Oh. I never thought of that.'

'Well, now you know how it is. Stop worrying, darling. Unless there's anything else?'

He didn't really want to ask that, but wanted to be sure, wanted to know exactly what she was thinking and feeling. Another little huffy sigh, more exasperated than worried he thought.

'No, nothing except female stuff, time of the month and all that. Don't you notice that I get a bit scratchy every so often?'

'Oh, poor darling. I'm sorry. And no, I think you're lovely all the time.'

Now he was rewarded by a little giggle and then she went on.

'But, I really don't think I'll go to the club on Wednesday, sorry.'

He felt deflated by that as he looked forward to Wednesdays which had become a regular part of their lives.

'OK. Can I come round and have coffee if I go down and play?'

'Yes, of course. Come whenever.'

They talked some more and she said she was going for a hot shower and an early night. He told her again he loved her and would look forward to seeing her tomorrow. When he had rung off, he sat thinking and wondering. He had made a hash of the Rome invitation, but he was weighing-up if he could suggest a weekend away before she took over from Steve. Having postponed his own holiday, he would welcome a change of scene and suddenly realised that he could use that as a reason. Then he thought he was being manipulative, trying to get her to agree to something because he felt the need for a break. However, hopes were dashed as soon as he looked at his working schedule for the coming weeks. Umm, not good. In fact, pretty bad as far as planning anything was concerned. This coming Friday, "Charity Auction." Ah, that time of year again. The auction was one of Max's initiatives that the firm was involved with and he knew he would be expected to go, make sure glasses were well topped-up, and press some flesh, hoping to loosen bidders' wallets for the good causes which were being supported. It would go on pretty late, drink would flow, so he had better stay up in London. Pity.

Wednesday was not a particularly nice day, typical July, fine but on the cool side, not what you would really like for mid-summer. As weather it was alright but could do better, he thought. He was in two minds about playing tennis and in the end, decided not to. But as he was going out anyway, thought he would call in at the club, put in a token appearance and see what, if anything, was going on. He knew he would be greeted by a chorus of disapproval for not playing, but he would deal with that. When he arrived, he felt vindicated as there weren't many people down at all and he was pleased not to have bothered. He found Alice in the pavilion, had a chat and in answer to her question about the weekend and whether he would be down then, told her that he had something on in London and wouldn't be down on Friday, but might be on Saturday, he didn't really know. He thought Alice gave him a sort of meaningful look and he wasn't sure why, but he continued the conversation and thought he ended up saying that he wouldn't expect to be down until the following week.

'And then it'll be nearly August,' Alice exclaimed, 'I don't know where the year is going to.'

'Do many people still come in the holiday season?'

George had just joined them and he took up the question.

'Oh, it gets a bit hit and miss. Sometimes there's the usual crowd and other times no-one. But we try to come down regularly as we get a few visitors coming in for a game as well.'

That turned the conversation to holidays and Alice started to quiz him about his plans and intentions. Again he thought she seemed to have some hidden agenda in the questioning, but told her that he had no plans as he had postponed his August holiday dates and hadn't yet settled on alternatives. Not wanting to be drawn any further into this line of conversation, Tom looked at his watch, professed himself surprised at the time, explained he had only popped in to say hello and was now off. Making swiftly for the door, he managed to pre-empt any questioning as to what he was doing next.

'Hello you.'

Gabriella, with slightly damp hair, opened the door and let him in, standing in the hall and smiling a bit apologetically at him.

'Sorry about sounding such a wimp last night. I'm really OK; take no notice of my little rants and moans.'

He scooped her into his arms.

'Good. I don't want this lovely girl to be hurt or in pain or anything nasty. But I can't do much about the fact that you're female, except be very thankful for it. And you smell like a garden of flowers.'

He kissed her, breathing in the scents of freshly-washed hair and the musky, heady perfume that was permeating her skin.

'What's the scent?'

He was kissing her neck, her ears, wanting to go on and on and on, until...

'It's called Byzantine Shade.'

'Mmm. I'll buy you litres of it, you can bathe in it and...'

'Stop, stop, stop,' she laughed, pushing him gently away. 'Now, practicalities, do you still want coffee or have you changed your mind?'

'I'll have Byzantine Shade, no sugar, please!'

'I'll take that as a yes to coffee. Come on, into the kitchen and we'll get the kettle on while you simmer down.'

She gave him the luxury of one more kiss and then led him firmly through the hall.

'You don't look as though you've played tennis.'

He sat on a chair while the kettle was boiling and she was measuring coffee into mugs.

'No, but I did pop in and show my face, not many people down so I was glad I hadn't bothered.'

The coffee was ready and he took both mugs from her and stood back for her to lead the way into her sitting room. But she suddenly stopped.

'Nearly forgot, went to the bakers in the lunch hour. Do you fancy a piece of cake?'

He looked at her.

'Oooh yes please, you know what they say about the way to a man's heart being via his stomach.'

She gave him an arch look and then reached for a knife, cutting two pieces of cake and putting them on plates.

'Personally, I think the route might be a bit different!'

He knew exactly what she meant and they both giggled.

'Go and I'll bring these.'

While they were eating and drinking, he remembered his idea.

'I was thinking about us going away for a weekend before Steve goes on holiday, but I've looked at my diary and can't do it. Sorry, I wanted you to have a nice, relaxing couple of days somewhere special.'

'Oh, that was sweet of you, perhaps later.'

He was delighted she had at least accepted the idea and told her about the Charity Auction and the fact he would be away on Friday night.

'Ah, so one of our financial institutions is doing good deeds this Friday.'

'Yes, very good ones. If there's anything that looks unusual, I just might buy it for you, but I don't think we're supposed to bid, so you're safe! Although, you don't really like me buying things for you, do you?'

'No, it's not like that.'

She was quite upset by his remark.

'You're a very generous person, Tom. Very. But I just find it difficult to accept really expensive stuff which I don't need and I'm sorry if it seems ungrateful, because I don't mean it to be.'

'But presents are about being nice-to-have, not necessities.'

'I know. But...' she pulled a sad face, 'it's just not what I'm used to.'

'OK. Well, I shall just have to use my judgement and buy, if I can, before asking. And,' he had a smile developing which broke into a broad grin, 'come here, you'll just have to make it up to me in other ways.'

That made her laugh and she got up from her chair and joined him on the sofa.

'Now, let's see,' he was slipping buttons undone, 'what colour bra tonight?'

'Tom Scotford, you're incorrigible and...' she got no further as he was kissing her and it was so good, she just had to relax and not bother where this might lead, as his hands were caressing, exploring and making her whole body tingle and respond to his touch.

'Oh, you're so gorgeous. Gorgeous Gabriella.'

And he ran his fingers through her hair and then down her cheek, neck and traced a line round her breast, before burying his head in her cleavage and kissing her again. And it could go on and on she thought, because she was beginning to trust his judgement and her part-drunk coffee would just have to go cool.

On Friday, Gabriella decided to go to tennis, knowing that it might be one of the last evenings for a while as August and Steve's holidays were approaching. She also knew that Kris would be departing for a backpacking holiday soon and as she really enjoyed playing with him, hoped that he would be down as well. He was, and they had two outstanding games together, great laughs and some pretty good play. Tom would be impressed, she thought, and wondered how the auction was going and how much champagne, which he said lubricated the proceedings, he might have consumed by now. She also wondered if he would buy anything and had a moment's pure fantasy about a van arriving at her house with a pickled pig or an enormous pile of rubbish which was, in fact, a piece of modern sculpture.

It was about eight-forty and she had decided not to play any more. Standing in the pavilion, having packed her bag, she was about to go outside and join Alice and Su who were sitting out, chatting. She could hear their conversation, sporadically drifting through the open doorway.

'We shall miss Kris coming down and I expect he'll miss his tennis too.'

'Yes, he will. He was hoping Tom would be down tonight, but no luck.'

'No, Tom's not here. He's in London tonight.'

Alice sounded very confident of that fact Gabriella thought, and smiled.

'I expect he's seeing his girlfriend up there.'

'Really? I didn't know he had a girlfriend in London, but not surprising. I mean he's so gorgeous he could have girlfriends all over the place. How do you know?'

Gabriella was standing just inside the doorway immobile, an awful pain shooting through her stomach.

'Oh, when he first came down he told me and George that he would often be away for work or seeing a lady friend who still lived in London.'

Gabriella had her hand over her mouth because she felt as though she might retch. Then she made her feet move, picked up her bag and stumbled out of the doorway.

'Going?'

Su was looking at her.

'Yes, not feeling like playing any more, got a bit of a tummy pain. Goodbye.'

Alice was now looking solicitously at her.

'Oh dear. Hope it goes quickly. See you soon?'

'I don't know. Work's building up before Steve goes on holiday so probably won't be down much. See you sometime. Bye.'

The idea of coming down to the tennis club was becoming a horribly complicated thought. Get to the car, she told herself, get to the car. Get home. The pain in her stomach was so crippling she didn't know whether she could drive, but she made herself, almost on autopilot through the town, before falling out of the driver's seat and running up to her door, sobbing.

An hour later, lying on her bed, still in her tennis clothes, she had exhausted herself weeping. Then, slowly, she raised herself, sat up, peeled off her clothes, threw them in a heap and got into the shower.

'It doesn't matter if you cry in the shower,' she moaned to herself, 'it doesn't show.'

That started her off again; she had never felt this bad, should never have let herself be so stupid as to believe she would be the only woman in his life. Never should have trusted that it could work when he was so special and could have his pick of anyone he wanted. She looked in the steamy mirror: wet bedraggled hair, red puffy eyes.

'Of course you're not good enough for him, why did you ever think you might be?' she wailed.

It was a long, largely sleepless night.

CHAPTER 10

Early on Saturday morning she got up and made some tea, bringing it back to bed for the sheer comfort of it. The plan had been that Tom would text her when he got on the train so she would know roughly what time he would be home and go round. They had agreed to spend a quiet day in the garden, if it was fine, while Tom recovered. But what was her plan to be now? By mid-morning she had made her decision. She would go to his house and confront him. Then she vacuumed robotically, waiting for the text.

By mid-afternoon, Tom was in his sitting room, complete with a throbbing head which spoke to him of about four glasses of champagne too many, when he heard the front door close. He opened his eyes, at least looking forward to seeing his lovely girl and spending a relaxing time out in the garden.

'Hello, darling,' he stopped, stunned by the figure who was standing in the doorway.

'Gabriella,' he was scrambling from his chair in fright, 'what's the matter? What's wrong?'

He thought someone must have died. She looked awful, pale, crying, almost dishevelled. She stood, uncertainly and then in a voice that was so ferocious it shook her frame, 'You've got another girlfriend, I'm not the only woman in your life, Tom Scotford.'

The words ricocheted round the room, hurting his head and it took him a moment to understand them.

'What makes you think that? Where's this come from?'

'Answer me.'

It was an anguished scream and tears were spilling down her face.

'You are the only woman in my life.'

He was shouting now. Then more quietly, 'Gabriella, you are my girlfriend, the only one. Why are you doubting it?'

'You've got a lady in London according to Alice.'

'Bloody Alice. Sorry. What does she know about my life?'

He was shouting again and there was an awful hammering inside his head.

'She said you told her when you joined.'

'Hell, I'd forgotten.'

'So it is true?'

She was rocking backwards and forwards, bunched fists scraping the wetness from her cheeks.

'NO, no, it's not.' Please, Gabriella, come and sit down. Please.'

He walked slowly towards her, reached for her arm and pulled her into the room and towards the sofa. Her body was taut and she was sobbing so violently he realised he had never, ever, seen anyone so upset.

'Now,' he held her in his arms, found his handkerchief for her, 'it's all alright. Everything's alright.'

He realised there was no point in launching into an explanation until she was calmer, so he stroked her hair, made soothing noises and waited for her to quieten.

'I'm making your shirt all wet.'

'Doesn't matter, it'll be more wet in the wash. Now, can you listen while I tell you how this misunderstanding came about? Because that's what it is.'

She took a ragged, wet breath and nodded.

'Good.'

And he told her about having had a London girlfriend when he first joined the club, but not having one now because they had parted company some months ago. He didn't elaborate, but made up his mind to answer any questions honestly.

'Gabriella, look at me, please.'

She raised her head.

'Do you believe what I'm saying? There is no-one else.'

'Yes, yes, I do believe you and,' she was sobbing again and he could just make out the words as she sank her face into the hankie, 'I shouldn't have doubted, you've given me no reason to, I'm so, so sorry I...'

'Sshh. No more. Listen. I work odd hours at times and it would be easy enough to live a sort of double life, play home and away as it were. But I don't. And I don't because I love you. Now, deep breaths please, mop up these tears. It's all over, nothing to worry about.'

It took another five minutes or so for the tears to subside into little hiccoughing snuffles and then with a final, deeper breath, she sat up.

'I'm OK now. It was just...'

'No more.'

He wasn't going to let her agonise any further as his head seemed to have some sort of percussionist lodged behind his eyes.

'Now, I need to get some fresh air and its warm enough outside, so come on, we'll have a lounger each and a bit of a sleep. Oh, I need a couple of Paracetamol as well.'

'Tom, I forgot about the auction.'

She looked at him, full of concern for him now and gently ran her fingers down his cheek. 'Are you a bit under the weather? Was there a lot of champagne?'

'The answer is yes to both, but it's self-inflicted and I shall recover, but I think an hour's sleep will help and I imagine, if I know anything about Gabriella Devonshire, she perhaps didn't sleep too well last night either. So, a bit of recuperative rest and whoever wakes up first, makes tea.'

He must have gone out like the proverbial light as when he woke, looked at his watch, it was later than he expected and the lounger next to his was empty. His head still felt muzzy and not quite belonging to his body, but the crashing hammer-blows had gone, thank goodness. He was about to get up when he saw Gabriella walking from the kitchen with mugs on a tray.

'That looks so good. Thanks. How do you feel? I'm recovering slowly but nicely.'

'I'm better now, thanks.'

She handed him a mug.

'And I'd like to hear about the auction please.'

It was true, she did look better, although still bearing the marks of crying on her face. As he drank his tea, Tom told her that he had seen something he really wanted and had wondered how he could go about buying it. Then finding someone he knew well enough to ask a favour, he got the friend to bid and buy it and gave him a cheque for his purchase when Max wasn't looking!

'You must have really wanted it. What was it, have you got it here?'

'I'm not telling you what it was because it's still packed up and I want to decide where to put it. I'll show you tomorrow.'

'Oh.'

'Patience will be rewarded and it's something for me, so I didn't actually buy you anything.'

'Good.'

He roared with laughter until his head started to complain, amazed at this girl who just didn't automatically expect gifts to be bought for her. Then she told him about the pig and rubbish fantasy and laughing made his head hurt again. But he didn't mind, she seemed to have recovered and, with a bit of luck, things could settle down again. Also, he wondered whether, when she reflected on her reaction, as he knew she would, she might realise something about the depth of feeling and emotions which Alice's comment had ignited. It could, in a strange way, have shown her something important, help them on their journey. But then he remembered that Steve would soon be away and the road might get increasingly rocky again.

On Sunday they went out for lunch and then a walk. She often mentioned work issues and the fact that Steve would soon be away, but at least she was diverted because there was something she was waiting and eager to see when they got back – his auction purchase.

'Where did you decide to put it?'

She was angling for information because he hadn't given any indication of what he had bought.

'Well, I had two choices. It could go in my bedroom or in the sitting room.'

'Really?' And where is it?'

'In the sitting room. I decided it was a bit too hazardous to have it in my room.'

He had a grin on his face and was deliberately feeding her curiosity.

'But,' he was opening the front door, 'come in, close your eyes before you get to the sitting room and I'll tell you when you can open them.'

'Will do.'

She closed her eyes, and he could see, was enjoying the game. He walked her through the hall and into the sitting room.

'Now, you can look.'

'Oh my word.'

'What do you think?'

They were looking at a picture. It showed a young blonde girl, standing by a river or a lake, one foot stretched towards the water, about to test the coldness. The colours were soft and pale, except for the bright red splashes of nail polish on her toes. The painter had captured a three-quarter view, side and back of the girl, who was nude.

'I think I can see why you liked it.'

'Does it remind you of anyone?'

She looked at him, smiling shyly.

'I can't really answer that.'

'And,' he put his arms round her, circling her and kissing her neck, 'one day, my own, nude blonde will be in the bedroom. One day.'

'Oh, I see.'

Work was pretty full-on during the week and Tom couldn't see any way of getting home early, not even on Friday. He was a bit aggravated about it because this was the last fortnight before Gabriella was left in charge of the office and he really wanted to spend as much time as possible with her. He still didn't know why she got so stressed about the idea of being in charge and could only think that in the way she had shown with something as unimportant as tennis, she was always striving for perfection. Then he wondered whether just a nice day out on Saturday would be possible. Do not assume, a warning voice told him, but he thought he would be ready with a possible plan if she would agree.

On Wednesday, Gabriella decided to go and play, knowing that she wouldn't have much time, energy or inclination next week or the one after. She didn't intend to stay long and, if Tom got home before nine, she would call in for coffee. The first person she saw when she arrived was Alice who was already out on court, and she felt her anger rising. Then she realised that she must steady her emotions and remember that Alice had only spoken what she believed to be true. Up until now she had not found the courage to ask Tom about the London lady-friend, but had a real sense that she needed to know something about her and wondered if Alice actually knew anything.

'Hi, Gabriella.'

Mike was standing in the doorway, watching her approach. That was good, she liked Mike and he was easy to talk to.

'Hello yourself. No Kris?'

'No, you've got to put up with me, I'm afraid. He's off backpacking and so far we know he's reached Spain. You ready to play? Not many down tonight but we can make up a four now I think.'

Not many more people arrived that evening and Gabriella didn't have to play terribly well, but hadn't much chance to sit out either. A couple of visitors had turned up, so the club members did their best to mix in and play as many games with them as possible. When she got a moment to check her phone and saw that Tom had just got back, she announced that the next foursome would be her last. She also announced that she wouldn't be down much in mid-August, but would look forward to playing after that when, she had been reminded, Kris would also be back.

'So that's good timing, my favourite partner getting back when I shall be returning to action.'

She said that deliberately, still no-one making any connection between her and Tom and possibly the idea that he possessed a girlfriend had deflected attention in a way they hadn't imagined. She thought that it might be a good idea to leave Alice and Su in ignorance.

Driving through the town she started smiling. She was about to encounter her alter ego hanging on Tom's sitting room wall! She could see the likeness even though she wouldn't actually acknowledge it in words and had heard his contention that the picture of the nude blonde would do until he got the real thing into his bedroom. She wondered about whether he had taken the London girl to bed and suspected he had. She opened the front door and stepped inside.

'It's only me.'

'Good. I wasn't expecting or hoping for anyone else.'

He crossed the room and took her in his arms, kissing her until she broke free, needing to catch some breath. Then she walked solemnly up to the picture.

'Good evening, blonde girl. Hope you're being good, not leading Tom here astray.'

He laughed, grabbing her again.

'I've told you, that's for you to do. And,' he threw her down onto the sofa, 'I think a bit of going astray is called for before anyone gets a drink made.'

She allowed time for them to kiss, but before things got too hectic, looked at him seriously.

'Tom, can I ask you about your previous girlfriend?'

He had actually been expecting the question to be raised.

'Of course, if you want to know.'

'I think I need to know, but couldn't really explain why. What was her name?'

'Caroline.'

'And what was she like?'

He held her closely.

'That's easy to answer. She was almost an exact opposite of you. Tall and dark-haired.'

'And were you very in love with her?'

He answered without hesitation.

'No, I'm sure I never was. It was a sort of social partnership which suited us both at the time. But it wasn't love.'

'How did it end then? Who ended it, Caroline or you?'

He stopped and smiled at her.

'Hey, I didn't realise you wanted a blow by blow account. I'd better give you the whole nine yards, because some of it's quite amusing, at least I thought so. Right, let me set the scene, it was a Friday evening and I had asked Caroline to meet me for dinner, and I'll give you a precis of the main stuff.'

The restaurant was over half full and he ordered a double gin and tonic while he waited. As expected, exactly at eight, he saw a flash of magenta material and Caroline, immaculately presented as always, was making her way across the floor towards the table. As usual, he could see the effect she had on others in the room. He rose, took her hands and kissed her lightly on each cheek. She sat opposite, placing her handbag on a spare chair.

'Tom, good to see you. It's been so long since you've been seen in town the rumour is going round that you may have emigrated.'

He smiled, registering the first barb in the throwaway remark.

'No, just don't live here and like to get out as soon as I've finished work.'

He knew that Caroline had been totally against his move to the "sticks" and he wondered if she had guessed that he had an ulterior motive as well as the growing dislike of city living.

'Well, each to his own and as I see you are settled with a drink, I'll look at the wine list please.'

He passed it to her and waited.

'Nothing very appealing, but' she turned and summoned a waiter with a brief wave, 'a bottle of the Chablis and make sure it's at the correct temperature.'

Tom smothered a laugh at the look on the waiter's face. He couldn't have registered more shock if she'd asked him if he'd murdered his granny. This was the Caroline he had known for the best part of two and a half years, extremely clever, a successful lawyer and one for whom nothing ever seemed perfect, good enough or even acceptable.

'So, how are things?

Her voice brought him hurtling back to the present.

'You look a bit well-travelled.'

She had noticed the suit.

'Anywhere nice?'

He was about to tell her, but the maître d' was bearing a bottle of wine towards the table and had a glint of battle in his eyes. Mercifully, she accepted it and, he noticed, as he gave her a brief outline of his trip, managed to get through half a large glass in pretty quick time. He presumed she was satisfied with its temperature. They ordered and he steered the conversation on to her job, her brother, whom he quite disliked, and the doings of a few mutual acquaintances whose names he *managed to dredge out of his memory.*

They had finished their starters and he hadn't bothered to ask how her food was when she looked at him.

'So how's the house refurbishment? When's the party, it's about time you had one.'

He thought quickly, getting away from Caroline had been his ulterior motive and somehow he had managed to convince her for the last year that the place was still undergoing various repairs. What had he said last time about the state of the house? Better think of something new.

'I think it needs the roof looking at.'

It wasn't a complete lie because he had identified a few tiles which needed re-pegging and he thought he might get one of those firms in to pressure-wash the moss and algae off as well.

'Goodness, I don't think that was one of your better purchases, Tom. Not like you.'

They were in a lull, waiting for their main courses to arrive, and Tom realised that this was his opportunity. He made himself sound very calm and rational as he spoke.

'Perhaps you've never really understood my reasons for moving and that brings me to something important I want to tell you. Why I suggested meeting in fact.'

He could see he now had her full attention and she was listening with her lawyer's training, ready to sift and weigh whatever he said.

'I'm going to say that I think we've come to the end of our relationship and it would be better if we finished now, rather than let it drift, as it has been doing.'

She looked back at him calmly. He had known she wouldn't make a scene and he waited.

'Tom, that wasn't what I expected as your opening gambit. That's a bit out of the blue if you don't mind my pointing it out.'

She was very controlled and he could sense that her next move would be designed to get him on the back foot just as he had ambushed her.

'I'm sorry you think that way.'

She reached across the table and laid a hand lightly over his. She was smiling. It was like waiting for a snake to attack.

'Tom, darling, you really don't need to worry on my account, I can cope with the somewhat sporadic nature of the way things are. It's absolutely no problem. Don't worry about it any more.'

This was going to be like a game of chess.

'That's very gracious of you, but you don't quite understand. I don't want us to continue, it has no future.'

She looked momentarily angered and then the neutral, lawyer's expression returned.

'I obviously don't agree with your stance on this, so what's going to happen about August? I was going to ask you what you've done about our holiday arrangements.'

This one he was ready for.

'The answer is nothing because something has come up and I'm changing my dates at work. I'm not sure when I'll be taking leave yet, depends how things go.'

He expected she would accept this as a not unknown, if inconvenient, change and before she could reply, he continued.

'I know that's not totally good for you, but hope that this amount of notice will mean you can arrange an alternative.'

She sighed as though he couldn't possibly understand the

inconvenience he was actually causing her.

'Umm, well, that's what I shall be forced to do, but it's hardly what I was expecting.'

'Well at least the tourist industry is awash with late deals at the moment. One of our staff got a fantastic all-inclusive package to a Greek island and is flying out on Sunday I believe.'

She gave him a pitying look, poised with her wine glass in mid-air.

'Well, that's alright if you care for that sort of thing.'

'Oh, I thought it sounded wonderful, just the sort of thing that would be nice to do.'

She raised her eyebrows, looked at him and put the glass to her lips. Stop it, he warned himself, don't start trading barbs, keep it neutral. Fortunately the main courses were arriving and he reached out and poured himself a glass of wine, noting that it was excellent. They both ate, silently for a moment then, to his amazement, she suddenly set off on a different tack.

'Tom, tell me, how many hours on average do you work in a week?'

He started to brush aside the question, but she simply repeated it. He did a rough calculation for her. Although he thought he could see where she was heading, he decided to wait again and continued to eat. She pushed the food round her plate for a while, another habit which irritated him, because in a few minutes she would complain it was cold and therefore inedible and then looked up.

'You've just been to Amsterdam and the last time we met, you were off to New York I think it was. Working the hours you do and making this mad dash backwards and forwards from your less than habitable house on a daily basis, plus having to cancel your summer break, leads me to believe that you're burning yourself out Tom. All this talk about us ending is a symptom of a sort of midlife crisis.'

She ate a little of the food. Tom was trying not to smile because he quietly thought that was hilarious.

'Oh, come on. I'm thirty seven, that's not exactly middle-aged you know.'

'Nevertheless, I think you're in a bit of a low state, both physically and emotionally by the sound of things, and so I'll tell you what we'll do.'

He thought he had made it plain what they were going to do, but knew she was in summing - up mode and let her continue.

'You just try to take it a bit easier for a few weeks and I really think you ought to see the doctor.'

She conveyed a few more morsels onto her fork. Tom now had to stifle a huge laugh; he might be occasionally tired, but was as fit as he had been ten years ago. Then he pulled himself together and managed to look suitably attentive as she continued.

'Then, sometime next month, I'll give you a ring and we'll meet up and I think you'll be feeling differently by then.'

She took a long time deciding whether there was anything else on the plate worthy of consideration and chose half a scallop. He was about to refute the lot when he remembered an old negotiating ploy; give up something unimportant to the opposition if you're achieving what you want.

'Caroline, thanks for the advice. I will see the doctor, have a check-up and see what he says.'

He knew, unequivocally, he would not change his mind about them splitting up now that he had actually told her.

'Good. Now, let me see whether a dessert will be any better than this was.'

She had dealt with him and, he thought, removed him to the side of her life for a month, rather as she was now removing the dinner plate to one side of the table. But he was wrong.

'Tom,' she was looking at him with an intense expression, 'tell me the truth, have you got someone else?'

He met her challenging gaze.

'No, Caroline, I'm not seeing anyone else.'

'There.'

He'd told her as much as he could remember from what had actually happened that night.

Gabriella looked at him as he ended the story.

'You didn't tell her about me?'

'I hadn't asked you out then. Don't you remember saying that my telling you I loved you came out of the blue? Well, I'd been so preoccupied by finishing with Caroline, and I'd let it drag on much longer than it should have done, I just failed to notice the beautiful girl who had suddenly come on the scene.'

'Ah,'

She was nodding as though something had just fallen into place.

'That's why I didn't see it coming. I couldn't understand at the time why I hadn't.'

'You didn't see it coming because in many ways, neither did I. But when I did, it was like being hit by an avalanche – I was totally bowled over.'

'So,' a mock-severe look was creeping across her face, 'I got you on the rebound, did I?'

He laughed.

'Not really. I wasn't in love before I met you and that's the truth.'

'And did she really never stay here?'

'No. I managed to keep my home as my private bolt-hole. Don't quite know how, except that I managed to convince everyone in London that there was a lot of work to do on the house and I was sort of camping here. They found it very odd of course, but it worked.'

'And was she upset? I mean was she in love with you?'

He thought for a moment.

'I don't really like myself for saying this, but she was in love with my bank account and what I could buy her. I'm not sure about me as a person. I don't think she will grieve at our parting too much.'

Gabriella's face suddenly lit up – a eureka moment.

'Did you buy her a designer handbag by any chance?'

'No. I bought her about four. I can remember two Mulberry ones and there were at least one or two others.'

'Grief. No wonder I was such a surprise for you.'

He pulled her closer again and kissed her.

'Yes, my darling. You were a surprise. And once I got over the shock, a really, really lovely one. You're a giver, my darling, not a taker and it's one of the very many reasons I love you so much.'

She snuggled up to him.

'Tom, thanks for telling me all that. It helps me understand and now I can forget it. Oh.'

She had suddenly thought of something else.

'Will she contact you again?'

He noted the old anxiety spreading across her face.

'No. I wrote to her when I was in Scotland and posted it before I rang you with my out of the blue declaration of love.

She smiled and nodded as though she could now make sense of what had been such a conundrum.

'Well, another lot of water under the bridge, I think.'

'Good. And now we can move on and I'll tell you about some plans, if you agree, for a day out on Saturday, somewhere nice and relaxing.

She looked at him and smiled, 'Blonde girl says, thank you. That sounds nice.'

CHAPTER 11

It was only nine-forty-five and work was feeling a bit tedious. Tom acknowledged that he didn't usually feel that, but the previous weeks had turned into such an emotional roller coaster that the prospect of dealing with the intricacies of the commodities sector was not uppermost in his mind, if he were honest, on this particular Monday morning.

They had spent a great day out on Saturday: lunch and use of the leisure facilities at a very nice hotel and then they had gone back to Gabriella's house. Relaxing after a cup of tea, he had kissed her and explored her beautiful body and had met no resistance as he laid aside more and more of her clothing, so that at one delicious moment he believed she was going to let him continue and make love. But then a restraining hand had told him otherwise. He exhaled at the memory, but he had the feeling they were getting closer and soon...

'Oh, come on, enough.'

He switched to another screen on his computer. He needed to speak with Fredi, who should be back from leave, about a cryptic diary entry he had for Saturday week which just said "C.H." He had wracked his brains, but had no idea what it meant or even if it was something involving him. He hoped it wasn't. He buzzed her office.

'Hi Fredi. Good holiday?'

'Yes thanks. Back to work for a rest. We went to Disneyland.'

'Oh my, I bet the kids loved that.'

'They did. But, what can I do for you? I presume you haven't rung to see my holiday snaps?'

He laughed.

'No. I hope you can tell me why I've got a diary entry saying "C.H." on Saturday week. Haven't a clue what it is.'

'Tom, really.'

It was as much of a reprimand from Fredi as he ever got.

'It's Max's corporate hospitality event instead of Wimbledon this year.'

'Oh, right. I wondered why there weren't any Wimbledon tickets about in July. But what is it and am I supposed to go?'

'Tom,' slightly more exasperated, 'you've got an invitation card somewhere, because I sent them all out about two months ago.'

'Hell, could be anywhere, I'll look. But what is it?'

'It's a river cruise with dinner on the boat and a jazz band. You'll enjoy it.'

'I wanted to go to Wimbledon,' he moaned, actually meaning it.

'Sorry.'

He could hear her amusement at his petulance.

'Go and look for your invitation and tell me if you can't find it.'

'Thanks Fredi.'

Now, even more out of sorts, he started a lengthy search of his office until he found the invitation, looked at it and then had an idea.

The rest of the day was still boring and he spent quite a lot of time thinking about how he would introduce this idea to Gabriella, because the invitation stated, Mr Tom Scotford and Partner. On the plus side was the fact that they had really talked properly to each other about the Caroline business. Unsurprisingly, it hadn't taken her long to slot all the events into correct, chronological order but then he had been surprised when she told him about the change in his personality which people at the club had noted. Not for the first time he realised how transparent his feelings and emotions had been. On the minus side, this would come while Steve was away and he had already been warned that she would get tired and probably a bit short-tempered as she coped with the extra demands in the office. But, the event was on a Saturday, it sounded a fun thing to do and she might see it as a welcome distraction.

Later, as he drove home preparing how he would put it to her, he remembered the Romegate incident and, by the time he was parking in front of the house, determined that he would play it very low-key, simply tell her about the invitation and that he could take a partner. He noticed the light blinking on the answer machine as soon as he got through the front door and, before even going into the kitchen, pressed the 'play' button.

'Hello darling, just to let you know, Steve and I are working a bit late and then I'm going to have an early night. Catch up with you tomorrow. I'll phone you. Love and kisses to keep you going.'

He pressed delete. Never assume that things will turn out the way you have planned he thought, never assume. Ah well, an early night wouldn't do him any harm either.

They had agreed to try to get down to play tennis on Wednesday and Tom did manage to get away early. Gabriella turned up later and, he noted, seemed a bit lacklustre and not playing particularly well. There was none of her usual competitiveness on show, and he hadn't the heart to scold her for lack of effort. Her general lack of enthusiasm was a bit worrying, because he had made up his mind to tell her about the Saturday river cruise and ask her to come as his partner. At about quarter to nine, he heard her say that she wouldn't play anymore that evening and he knew that she would, when convenient, leave and go to his house. He had also heard her telling people that she would not expect to play much in the next two weeks due to work commitments. At the moment she was sitting chatting and he thought that he would take the chance to slip away first. He couldn't think of a reason why he wasn't staying, so hoped no-one would quiz him too closely. Once home, he put on the kettle and waited.

Having eventually made her own goodbyes and driven to Tom's house, Gabriella let herself in and walked through the hall to the kitchen.

'Tea or coffee?'

Tom was poised by the kettle ready to make whatever drink she chose; she opted for tea and sank onto a chair. He made her tea and handed her a mug.

'Here, you look as though you need this. I thought you looked a bit tired tonight, are you?'

'I think it's emotional tiredness as well as a bit physical.'

She was cupping both hands around her mug.

'Explain please.'

He sat opposite her with his own coffee and waited for her to elaborate. He was pleased that he had gauged the tiredness correctly and wondered if there was anything else. Between gulps of hot liquid she explained that as well as the normal tiredness of work and things building up, their personal journey had contributed as well.

'We've had such a strange, tense, enjoyable, all mixed-up few days of late that I'm probably feeling the effects a bit still.'

She was about to go on, but he wanted to check something out.

'Gabriella, you've told me that you worry about things. Are you worried about us, about things on this journey we're on?'

She looked a bit confused.

'Not worried in the usual way, no.'

'So, in what way?'

He paused, but she seemed unable to answer.

'Do you worry that I'm slightly older than you, for instance?'

'No, no. I mean, nine years is nothing.'

'Good. Then what about the fact that I work in London and am quite often away?'

'No, that's not a problem. Really not.'

She seemed to realise that some sort of explanation was needed.

'I suppose I worry about whether things will turn out OK, whether I'm the right person for you. What I would consider normal things in a relationship. But although this may sound totally illogical, they're not things that you need to worry about even though I do.'

He laughed. He sort of knew what she meant, but then she continued.

'But mainly, even though you've told me not to, I'm worrying about running the office when Steve goes on holiday.'

He reached over and took her hand, giving it a little shake. He was obviously not winning this particular battle yet.

'But you know you can do it, you've done it before and you've said that all the staff rally round.'

'I know,' her eyes were dark and she looked almost close to tears, 'but I still worry about it, even though I know I shouldn't.'

She drank the remains of her tea.

'Sorry,' a glimmer of a smile, 'I'll try to buck up a bit and not be such a misery.'

He decided that this was his opportunity and said that he had something to tell her about which just might be a bit of distraction therapy for her. She listened as he told her about the invitation, what it would be like and the fact that he could take a partner.

'I know this will be right in the middle of when Steve has gone on holiday but as it's a Saturday, it shouldn't affect work and may act as a bit of a diversion, perhaps. So, as I have to go, would you like to come with me?'

He wasn't surprised that she didn't answer straight away as she often tended to consider things before she replied. After a pause, she raised her head and looked at him, and he already knew the answer.

'Tom, thank you, but I don't want to accept. It's so kind of you, but the answer is no.'

She dropped her gaze and looked close to tears again. He reminded her that it was only a few hours on Saturday if she was worried about taking too much time out of her weekend.

'No, it's not the time involved that's the issue.'

'It would help me if you could explain what the issue is, but if you don't want to, then I accept that you don't want to come.'

Although he wasn't, he tried to sound calm and patient.

'As I've said, I have to go, it's sort of expected.'

She looked at him with a strained expression on her face, then reached out and took his hand. He could see her trying to choose the words to bring out her full and exact meaning, so that meant this was important. Finally she spoke, very softly, and as though she almost didn't want him to hear the explanation.

'It isn't that the trip would take up time or that I know I will feel even more tired by then.'

She paused again, looking into the middle distance.

'I can't see us as that sort of couple, going to a corporate function together. I can't see myself in that role and I'm so sorry to disappoint you like this.'

He got up, came round the table, kissed her gently and tried to reassure her that in the big scheme of things it didn't matter. He was remembering the Rome upset.

'Listen darling, don't be upset, we draw a line under it and move on. Yes?'

She nodded.

'You're so kind, I don't deserve you to be so good to me.'

He stopped her talking any more.

'Sshh, we've drawn a line. Now, you look pretty tired, so off you go and get a good night's sleep.'

He could hardly believe that he was voluntarily telling her to go home, but she looked absolutely whacked and he had heard her almost snap at George earlier in the evening. Nevertheless, he was aware that just as things had been going forwards, now suddenly, they were setting off in reverse. But, he told himself, he had to see this as a temporary setback and manage the next few weeks as best he could. He led her to the door and out to her car.

'Drive carefully, I'll ring you tomorrow.'

He kissed her lightly on the forehead and held the car door open for her.

Back in his kitchen he poured himself a brandy to go with his coffee and went through to the sitting room. In his mind, he heard his voice saying that in the big scheme of things it didn't matter. Of course it mattered. However he tried to dress it up as a temporary setback, this was crucial. If she couldn't see them as partners who could go to events together then what sort of partners could they ever be? Had she been telling the truth? Had he understood fully what she driving at? Was this how she felt now and it might change? Too many questions, he decided. When she was looking a bit less fragile, he would have to ask her what she really thought about their future partnership.

Things didn't improve much over the next few days. Gabriella and Steve worked late and she seemed to be keeping Tom at arm's length, saying she was not good company, too tired etc. He had suggested another nice day out on Saturday, but she had insisted it must be a day for her to catch up on housework, gardening and get herself sorted for the following week. He knew not to interfere or suggest he would come round and help.

On Saturday he didn't feel like doing anything much himself; he worked in the garden, ate a solitary meal and then sat out with a bottle of wine on the table beside him. He was aware that things had not gone quite as he had anticipated after he had made that phone call and told her he loved her. And he was, for the first time, beginning to doubt the chances of success. He had been so pleased that the Caroline thing had been resolved but then she had dropped that bombshell about not seeing herself as his partner. He remembered her telling Simon she didn't want a long term commitment and although he thought that had been a bit of a smokescreen to refuse him, now he was beginning to believe it might be very true. He had thought this was going to be easy, because he had imagined she would simply fall deeply in love with him just as quickly, well almost, as he had with her. But it didn't seem to be happening.

On Sunday, just after twelve, she rang and said she had slept well and given herself a bit of a talking-to. He was relieved but didn't dare ask whether the talking-to had included any change of decision about the river cruise and she didn't mention it either. He had worked all morning with Ken and between them they had dug out an enormous tree stump at the bottom of the garden. He told her about their efforts.

'As I think I've earned some relaxation, would you like to do anything this afternoon or evening, as long as it doesn't involve digging?'

He heard her laugh and she did sound in better spirits he thought.

'Do you know what I would like to do? I would like to have a walk along the canal by the "Boatman," and then have a meal somewhere.'

'Sounds good enough to me. Can I suggest that we have say one drink in the "Boatman" and then come back here for a meal, as I've just looked in the fridge and it still seems to be rather full? But if you want to eat out, then we can just stay at the pub. Your choice and either is OK.'

She responded immediately.

'If you've got food, then I'm happy to help you eat it, so we can skip the pub altogether and I'll bring some wine.'

While they were preparing the meal and having a glass of wine, Gabriella started to scuffle in the depths of her large, canvas bag. She brought out a box and put it on the kitchen table.

'That's for you, it's a present and you're to read the card with it.'

He put down his glass and walked over to look at the box she had put down. It was hand- made chocolates and the card simply said:

To the sweet man in my life: a little extra sweetness to make up for any lack of mine.'

Before he could speak, she had slipped her arms round him and kissed him. He held her close, feeling better than he had done for days.

'Where did you get those on a Sunday morning?'

'After I'd rung you I went to a Farmer's Market in a village the other side of Cadmore. I sometimes go there, and there's a lady who has a stall selling home made cakes and jams and she also does these chocolates.'

'You went there specially?'

She nodded.

It was when she did something like this, so spontaneously and lovingly, that he really couldn't imagine not having her in his life as his partner.

'Darling, darling, thank you. We'll have them with coffee.'

She sat down and gazed at him and he could sense that she really did want things to go well between them. Well, perhaps they would, but... Well who could know?

* * *

The August weather was wet, cool and windy and Gabriella was one of the few people to be pleased about that, because there was going to be virtually no tennis or anything social for her this week. Tom was keeping a low profile, watching her slight - or on one occasion, when the photocopier had blown up - huge mood swings, and trying to offer her food and peaceful surroundings whenever she would accept them. He was still surprised that she worried so much about work, because he believed she was a very competent and conscientious person. It was interesting though that someone who generally appeared so outwardly confident could be anxious and worried. But he was becoming increasingly aware that she was quite a complex character. Thinking of the next few days, reminded him that on Saturday he would be going on the Corporate Hospitality do alone, but he knew that this wasn't a good time to re-open the question of what she had really meant by her refusal to go as his partner.

On Friday, when he checked his mobile on the train home, Gabriella had left a message to say that to celebrate getting to the end of Week One, she had come home a bit early and was going to play tennis; so she would see him later, if he could make it. When he arrived at the club, she was already there and wearing the skirt that he knew she particularly liked, which he hoped was a good omen. There were quite a few people down that evening and they only played in one foursome together, but he was pleased to see that she was on good form and he heard her laughing and joking and was himself on the receiving end of one or two really rasping forehands which she peppered at him with obvious pleasure.

Gabriella was really trying to enjoy the evening as she was delighted that they had got through Week One of Steve's absence without any major traumas. Alex had got the copier company in to replace the machine and everyone said the new copier was much better than the other one had ever been. But she had also remembered Tom's trip tomorrow and knew she had deeply disappointed him by refusing to go. She wasn't sure whether he had understood what she meant and she didn't know whether she had explained her reasons very well, but as neither of them had mentioned it again, she had never got round to revisiting the matter. And, even though they had a lovely time relaxing together after the tennis, it still remained a taboo subject.

On Saturday, spending a quiet day alone, she realised just how much a part of her life Tom had become and that she did miss him – quite a lot if she were honest. She thought about what they might have been doing together if this had been an ordinary Saturday and how really nice it was to have someone special, someone who took you out and shared things with you and generally, she had to admit, looked after you. Perhaps most of all, she missed the fun – life with Tom was a happy, carefree time and he did stop her worrying too much about things. She hoped he would enjoy the boat trip but wasn't going to think any further about it, because, well, because she'd opted out of this bit of his life and there could be things in it that she didn't want to think too hard about. Who else might be there for instance, like previous friends from London? Stop, she told herself, get on with the lawn next.

It was pouring with rain on Sunday but Tom didn't care because he had had a bit of a lie-in after getting back late from the boat trip and Gabriella had told him that to make amends for refusing the invitation, she would cook. The river cruise had been good fun, the music was excellent and the food passable. Several people had commented that he was on his own and a few asked after Caroline. Most seemed surprised that they were, in his words, "no longer an item." Whether it was that news percolating or not, he found that several apparently unattached ladies were very keen to introduce themselves and he realised just how easy it would be to have a one-night stand. But, he had also realised, he really didn't want to. Not yet, not until he had finally decided, if it came to it, that he and Gabriella weren't going to make a go of it.

At six o'clock, she arrived with a chicken and mushroom flan ready to go in the oven and some rather alcoholic chocolate brandy mousses. He was delighted to see her looking more like her normal self and then smiled as he wondered what 'normal' meant when considering Gabriella. He just hoped that they could get through the next week, and she could relax a bit more. He noted that she only asked a few details about yesterday and whether he had enjoyed it.

While they were drinking coffee, she suddenly looked up.

'After next week I can relax a bit and I shall be more bearable to live with, or slightly more,' she added with a grin.

'Come and do a bit of relaxing now,' he ventured, patting the edge of the large sofa. But in truth, he had learned over the last week, she was finding that impossible and all he could do was be very understanding, very undemanding and very patient. In fact he was amazing himself at times.

But, they survived the week. Tempers got frayed, but no-one, as he reminded her once, was getting injured or had died. And, unsurprisingly, life did progress without major incident to the last day of the working week.

On the Friday as she was driving back from work, Gabriella felt a strange mixture of elation, tiredness and concern in case next week would uncover something that had slipped or gone wrong, as well as huge frustration that she worried so much and it had such an effect on her. Having sorted out everything ready for Steve's return, she was a bit later than usual and was hitting pretty heavy, August holiday traffic. Once home, she decided to have a leisurely meal, a hot shower to hopefully get rid of a nagging tension headache and then to drive down to the club for a drink, but not to play. She was pretty shattered, but there was enough adrenalin from the relief of being able to hand back to Steve on Monday to give her the feeling that she could cope with the weekend.

She drove in through the gates at about quarter past eight and walked slowly from her car to the pavilion. Seeing Alice was sitting outside, Gabriella lowered herself onto a chair beside her.

'Aren't you playing tonight?'

Alice's tone was sharper than usual and Gabriella noticed that she looked angry, which was fairly unusual, and she wondered whether someone had upset her or George had done one of his infamous DIY repairs that had gone wrong. She explained that she had got home late after two weeks of really hard work and had decided that she wanted a totally relaxing evening for a change.

'That's a pity,' Alice was gazing even more angrily in the direction of the tennis courts, 'because we have a bit of a problem out there and poor Tom needs all the help he can get.'

Gabriella was amazed to hear Tom and problem mentioned in the same breath, as she hadn't even looked to see who was playing.

'Why, what's the matter?' she asked, finally locating Tom on court two, partnering a complete stranger.

'That young girl Lucy is what's the matter. Disgraceful behaviour, all over him, poor Tom must be so embarrassed by it.'

Gabriella had to smile at Alice's venom and anger, but turned her attention to what was happening out on court two. Lucy was about nineteen or twenty she guessed, highly made up even from a distance, with dark, shoulder-length hair which she kept tossing out of her eyes and a tee shirt which was stretched pretty tightly over an absolutely voluptuous bosom. But what was aggravating Alice so much was that she was apparently, with no disguise whatsoever, flirting outrageously with Tom on court. Gabriella watched, mildly fascinated, as the young girl managed to make sure she could touch him, smile adoringly at him, or get him to fetch balls for her so that she could look into his eyes (standing very close) and thank him. Once, she pretended to be slightly hurt so as to gain his attention (and be able to lean on him) and generally make her feelings and ambitions abundantly clear.

'Someone needs to do something about her,' hissed Alice, 'visitors should not behave like that.'

Gabriella, faintly amused that somehow visitors were expected to have a certain code of behaviour and, as always, feeling a bit irritated by Alice's excessive concern for Tom's welfare, thought that it was all rather funny.

'I'm sure Tom's big enough to look after himself,' she said, and then as an afterthought, 'he may even be enjoying it.'

That was a huge mistake. Alice immediately set off on a long description of Tom's excellent character and the fact that he would never, ever, enjoy such behaviour. Gabriella half listened, said yes or no occasionally and realised it was getting a bit chilly and she was really rather bored by this conversation. She had wanted to feel euphoric tonight, instead she felt scratchy, deflated and distinctly moody.

After about fifteen minutes, the game finished and the foursome left the court. Lucy had now linked her arm through Tom's and was chattering vivaciously to him, face upturned and eyes sparkling with desire. As soon as he saw Gabriella, Tom forcibly detached Lucy and came over to her chair.

'Aren't you playing tonight?' he asked with what she saw was a hint of desperation.

'No, just out for a bit of fresh air and relaxation,' she replied managing one of her brightest smiles.

He was about to say something else when George came up, looking nearly as thunderous as Alice.

'Would you like to play again?'

He had directed the question at Tom, but before he could reply, Lucy grasped his arm.

'Oh, please Tom, please let's play again, that was so enjoyable.'

She was gazing into his eyes, beseechingly, and Gabriella had a hard job not to burst out laughing in front of them, it was all so ridiculous.

'Oh, well, yes, um,' George was now on the back foot, not wanting to agree to her request, but aware that she was a visitor and must be offered the club's usual courtesy.

'Well, Alice and I could make up a four, I think everyone else wants to call it a day.'

She glanced at Tom, wondering if he was going to take up the offer of more nubile entertainment and noted that he was now looking quite uneasy.

'The light's going a bit, George, I'm not sure we would get many games in.'

Ah, she thought, not going to play ball. She smiled at the pun but did wonder quite why she was feeling so detached from this little pantomime.

'Tom's quite right.'

Alice had risen from her chair.

'I'm not going to play any more thank you, far too late.'

She looked triumphantly at Tom, having got him off the hook. But none of them had bargained for Lucy's tenacity. She opened her eyes wide and turned to face Tom.

'Then we'll just have to go up to the clubhouse and have a drink, and you'll have to escort me and show me the way as I'm just a visitor.'

Gabriella started to giggle as she could see Tom's normal courtesy being stretched to the point of making a rude refusal, but had to snap her features into serious mode as he turned towards her.

'Ah, Gabriella, as you've come for a bit of relaxation, why not join us for a quick drink?'

She didn't quite know why, perhaps it was because she was too tired to play the game, or had been so amused by the situation and Alice's angry reactions that she just decided to keep out.

'Thank you Tom, but I'm just about to leave. Another time perhaps.'

He looked absolutely stunned, turned away and rather icily told Lucy to follow him, but he couldn't stay long. Alice, eyes narrowing crossly, said a curt goodnight and hurried off in the direction of the retreating figures of Tom and Lucy, who had once again managed to secure her arm in his.

Gabriella chatted to a few people who had also come off court and then, rather earlier than she had anticipated, took her leave, driving through the town to Tom's house. She let herself in and put the kettle on. By now, on reflection, she was a trifle ashamed that she had amused herself at his expense and in truth didn't quite know why she had done it. So feeling a tiny bit guilty she sat down, hoping he wouldn't be too long. There was a real feeling developing within her that this evening was not going right, but that it should have been pleasant and so she ought to think what was happening and why. But her mind felt clouded, her head was still aching and she was aware that even the pleasure she had felt at the start of the evening and weekend had evaporated. Some inner sense was advising her to think clearly and carefully, but it was all too much effort and she didn't know where to start or why it was necessary. It was over half an hour before she heard him shut the front door and when he came into the kitchen, she could see he was angry.

'Well Miss Devonshire, I expected a bit more help from you, I must say.'

His voice was pure frost. She was already irritated by waiting longer than she had expected and now she was being attacked. So, fight or flight? She was on the attack immediately.

'I didn't think you particularly needed help; I thought you were quite capable of dealing with things on your own.'

He rounded on her.

'And no thanks to you, I had to.'

That struck a chord, she was absolutely incensed.

'May I remind you that you left me on my own to deal with Simon, I don't see much difference in the two incidents.'

He turned away.

'Is there any tea made?'

'No.'

She swept her bag off the table and stood up.

'I only waited till you got back to tell you that I'm going home.'

That was a totally unpremeditated remark, but suddenly wanting to do just that, she walked out of the kitchen and let herself out. Surprisingly, he didn't follow her, so she got into her car and accelerated away, feeling tears prickling behind her eyes and suddenly, anxiously, wondering what on earth she had done.

Once in her own kitchen, she made tea. She felt awful. They had never had a serious row since the Rome incident and it just seemed lately as though things kept going wrong. Tonight had been so unexpected, so odd and yet it must mean something about them both and their relationship. Now the sheer stupidity of her behaviour hit her, she thought she must phone him and at least apologise. But despite reaching for her bag to find her mobile, she stopped, and with a sigh, slowly walked upstairs clutching her mug of tea. The hot liquid was warming and calming and, as she drank it she tried hard to make some sense of what had just happened. If she started by apologising, then she would have to say why she had reacted like that and first she needed to sort out her thoughts and feelings. Then she had to understand just what was going on and where things were actually going. Where was their journey still heading? To do that, she needed time and space and an idea started to form. By the time she had finished her tea and got ready for bed, her planning was done. Swallowing a couple of Paracetamol and setting the alarm for seven the next morning, she climbed into bed and eased down under the duvet.

CHAPTER 12

When the alarm went off, Gabriella couldn't think why she had set it so early for a Saturday. But then, remembering last night's planning, she was out of bed, through the bathroom and dressed as quickly as possible. She had glanced out of the window before dressing and the day looked as though it would be fine and possibly quite warm as well; just right for the trip she had in mind. Throwing a few things into her large, canvas handbag, and picking up a road atlas, by seven-forty-five she was in the car, driving out of Upton Peploe. She didn't need a map for this part of the journey because all she had to do was to head south until she came to the coast. She was going to the seaside for the day.

The lack of traffic on the road was an unexpected pleasure, especially as it was the holiday season, and she felt in reasonably high spirits, enjoying the promise of the morning as she drove. Her headache had gone and she felt ready for the challenges she had set herself. While she drove, she reflected on her mission. After the upsets in the month so far, culminating in the Lucy episode last evening, she was going to spend the day thinking and sorting things out in her mind and making some decisions. But at the moment, there was no need for thinking, just enjoying the freedom of driving her car on a fine summer's morning. Calculating that it was going to take her at least an hour and a half to reach the little resort she remembered going to as a child, after about forty minutes, she decided to stop and put the top down. Once she had done that, she felt like a real, free spirit, the sun was shining and the wind blowing her hair.

As she had only stopped at breakfast time for a cup of tea and a Digestive biscuit, she pulled into a roadside cafe and had a huge mug of coffee. Then she was off again, now within striking distance of the coast. Her timings had been pretty accurate and she pulled into a parking spot along the esplanade just before ten o'clock immediately realising that in all honesty, she could hardly remember the place, but was delighted to find that the esplanade was directly alongside the beach with no high wall to block the view.

She sat in the driver's seat and watched. Couples with dogs were out walking, joggers of varying shapes and sizes puffed past and a few families were already staking their claim to a patch of the sand and shingle beach as the resort came to life. Most of all, she watched the motion of the sea. It had a powerful but rather hypnotic effect as the waves crashed in and broke into frothy foam and then skittered gently back again. After sitting for a while, she decided that she needed to stretch her legs and, putting the top back up, set off along the esplanade. She couldn't really see whether one direction was better than the other, but soon came to a little shop selling all the usual seaside paraphernalia but also newspapers. She bought a paper.

'Is there a cafe along here somewhere?'

The cashier, who probably answered the same question countless times a day, told her to keep on going and she would come to "The Sea Shell" a bit further up the road.

The cafe was indeed decked out like a huge, bright sea shell and there were packs of shells, shell mirrors and picture frames and a variety of shell jewellery on offer. Gabriella found a table and picked up a menu. When the lady who seemed to run it single-handed came to her, pad and pencil ready, she ordered a brunch sandwich and a pot of tea, then while she waited for her food, began to think about those things which needed sorting out in her mind. One was her refusal to go on the river cruise. Looking back, she concluded that she hadn't explained it well and wasn't sure Tom had fully understood what had made her refuse so instantly. She should have had the courage to explain that, in her heart of hearts, at that point in their journey, she couldn't become his public property with all that would have entailed. It would have jeopardised everything at that stage. There was also the sudden appearance of Simon. That had been deeply unsettling, but why? She mulled it over for a few minutes before realising that if they had continued to keep in touch after they had first met, then she might never have agreed to start on a journey with Tom. On the evening he had come back to talk to her, she had been sure that he was not the right man for her. But suppose they had kept in touch after their initial meeting and supposing Tom had not arranged to see her on exactly the same evening that Simon had arrived back, what then? So the question which needed an answer was whether the timing of all this had been crucially right or wrong?

'Here you are, dear, brunch and tea, enjoy them.'

Her train of thought broken, Gabriella looked down at her plate. The sandwich of egg, bacon, mushrooms and fried onions was huge! She poured a strong-looking cup of tea and set about the sandwich, putting the thinking on the back burner in her mind.

'That was really, really good,' she smiled at the lady as she paid her bill, 'and will definitely do for breakfast and lunch.'

'Here on holiday, dear?'

'No, just visiting, so what could I do or see here this afternoon, to make the day worthwhile?'

The lady told her that there wasn't really much to do, most people came just for the beach, but, there were sand dunes at one end of the esplanade and a walk alongside the river. Then, finding out that Gabriella had a car, she suggested the harbour at the other end of the bay where she could get a boat trip.

'Thanks, both of those sound good. Bye.'

She ambled slowly back to the car, got in and glanced at the paper for a while. The parking spaces were completely full now and the esplanade much busier. She noticed that the joggers had been replaced by pensioners, many of them arm in arm, many of them quite elderly and frail. The conversation with Simon flashed back into her mind and she remembered talking to him about the idea of lifetime commitment. How had he countered that? Yes, by saying that at the beginning of something you can't possibly know for certain how even the middle, let alone the end will look. Glancing out at the esplanade again, she wondered how certain any of these elderly folks had been fifty or sixty years ago. What might her life be like in twenty, forty years time and would Tom Scotford still be a part of it?

After a while she decided to do the walk through the sand dunes by the river, locked her car and set off. The dune area had less sand and more grass where it bordered the riverbank and, she could see, was a popular place for walking. Suddenly, her attention was caught by movement up ahead. It was a dog, bounding along, tail wagging, ears flying in the wind, chasing a stick being thrown time and time again by his owner. The black-spotted Dalmatian was playing. Within a few seconds, she had got to the place where the dog's owner was standing.

'Excuse me, but your dog is so beautiful, I just had to come and say hello. What's his name?'

'He's called Blackstock, but careful, he's been in the river and he's very wet.'

The dog bounded towards her, stopped, stood in front of her and shook a shower of droplets from his coat. They were like jewels flashing in the sunshine. Despite the risk to her clothes, Gabriella dropped to her knees and felt the wet muzzle bunt her hand and saw the deep, brown, almost laughing eyes, looking playfully at her.

'I'm afraid all he wants to do is play,' sighed the owner, 'no sense of responsibility as a guard dog or anything useful.'

'I think he probably has the right idea, and thank you for introducing him. He's wonderful.'

Blackstock wagged his tail, looking hopeful that this young stranger might play, but instead she turned away, retracing her steps and thinking about that wonderful animal. She had thought about getting a dog on several occasions since she moved into her house, but had never quite decided that it was a good idea. As she walked slowly to the car, she thought about Blackstock and smiled at his exuberance and sheer sense of freedom. And those melting brown eyes just asked to be loved.

Driving out of the main resort she found a steep road down to the harbour with a little car park at the top and, leaving the car there, walked down. Once in the harbour area she found what she was looking for, a board advertising boat trips and, even better, a small pleasure boat with about twenty people already aboard. Buying a ticket from a tanned and crinkled-faced mariner, who helped her clamber aboard, she selected a seat under a bit of canvas roofing. She hadn't brought any sunscreen or a hat, but thought that under the shade with her sunglasses on, she would be OK and also hoped that the sea was going to be calm, as it would be pretty embarrassing to throw up. The boat waited another ten minutes and then with a last call for any more passengers, slipped its moorings and they were heading for the open sea. Once out of the shelter of the harbour, the waves were bigger and the wind whipped her hair in all directions, but she didn't mind at all. It was exhilarating. She looked back at the coast, trying to see the places where she had been earlier in the day, but it took her some time to work out where things were on the land. Yes, she thought, the view is different because I'm in a different place now. A different perspective was giving a different view of things. It wasn't a terribly profound revelation, but today, she thought, it did have significance and she needed to remember it.

The trip lasted an hour and a half and when she got back to her car, Gabriella felt the need for a drink. As she had enjoyed "The Sea Shell" and it was the only cafe she'd seen, she decided to go back and hope to find a parking space somewhere within walking distance. Cruising up and down for about ten minutes, she was rewarded with a space near enough to walk back. As soon as she entered, the lady recognised her and was pleased that the boat trip had proved a good recommendation.

'What can I get you this time, dear?'

Gabriella knew exactly what she wanted.

'Please may I have a pot of tea and a piece of fruit cake?'

While she waited, she knew that this was going to be her last period of thinking time before she headed back; so now, she had to concentrate on the questions and, more importantly, the answers. Her order appeared almost instantly and as she cut the wonderfully moist cake into small pieces, she tried to get her head round the final thing that had been bugging her, in the back of her mind, all day. The final piece of the jigsaw was Lucy.

Pouring the tea, deep in thought, she bit into the cake. She knew that somehow all the pieces would fit together if only she could make them. Some things had become clearer today, but something was still eluding her. She drank her tea, thinking hard, getting everything lined up in her mind and just had to find how that last bit fitted in. Suddenly, it all became clear. That was the key, that elusive piece she had been searching for, and finally, she had the answer. It was so simple. Pouring a second cup of tea, she took a deep, satisfying drink and knew she could go back now.

She sauntered along the esplanade, savouring the sights and sounds. Dropping down onto the sea wall, she sat, taking one last look at the beach. The tide was further in now and some of the families with small children were beginning to pack up. Seagulls called to each other with their harsh, metallic cries and the waves continued their relentless, rhythmic pounding of the shingle. Then, with a little smile, she rose, turned towards her car, saw the lights wink their customary welcome and prepared for the return journey.

Tom was sitting in the garden working on some notes for a series of meetings coming up in the week when he saw her step out of the kitchen doorway. His heart jolted with relief, because he had spent most of the morning phoning and going round to her house, but she had gone. It was almost like Rome all over again. He had also spent some time thinking about what might happen next. He knew he had given this his best shot, he wanted this relationship to work, he wanted Gabriella so much, had tried to be patient, not rushing her, wanting to make her happy. But he still wasn't certain if she loved him enough to want him in her life for always.

After a moment, framed in the doorway, she started to run across the grass. Scrambling from the lounger and scattering the notes around his feet, he was just balanced and ready when she launched herself into his arms.

'Tom, Tom, I'm back. I'm sorry I went away, but I'm back, really back.'

He held her and looked into her face. She looked different, changed in some way, but he didn't know why.

'You haven't really been away from me, my darling, just temporarily missing for ten hours, but at least you're back now, and safe and OK.'

He hoped she was OK. She was breathing hard, but that might just have been the sprint across the lawn.

'I've had such a day.'

She paused as though remembering it and then looked up at him.

'I've been to the seaside.'

'You've been to the seaside, on your own?' he asked incredulously.

She nodded.

'Well, you'd better come in and tell me all about it.'

He led her into the house, discovered that she wasn't hungry and sat her down on her favourite corner of the sofa. He had feared the worst, but she seemed fine, not like she had been last night and he really didn't know what was going on, why she had gone to the coast on her own. Lowering himself onto his recliner where he could look at her, try to judge her expression, he was ready to listen. Time to find out, he thought, and hoped his normal optimism wasn't going to end up crushed and broken in pieces.

'So, tell me anything you want to about this adventure of yours.'

He could sense that somehow this day trip had been important, although he now felt afraid again of what the outcome might be.

It was as though verbal floodgates opened. She started with her journey from Upton Peploe and described what she had done in astounding detail. He heard about the roadside cafe, the esplanade, the joggers, the beach and the families.

'But then I saw lots of pensioners walking along and I remembered what I had said to Simon.'

Tom was listening, trying to gain clues from this mass of remembered detail and the fact that Simon appeared to have risen again out of nowhere was unnerving.

'Simon told me that sometimes you have to take risks, you can't always plan for the future and expect to know exactly what will happen.'

'Oh, right.'

He relaxed and tried to breathe a bit more regularly instead of holding his breath. Well, that seemed OK, he thought, nothing too disastrous there. Next she described "The Sea Shell" cafe and exactly what she had eaten and all the goods for sale and then her face took on a new expression and she started to tell him about a Dalmatian dog.

'Tom, he was so beautiful and he came up to me and showered me with drops of water and then he put his muzzle into my hand and looked at me.'

Her face was ecstatic with the memory.

'His name was Blackstock and he had these wonderful brown eyes and he was so adorable.'

For a bizarre instant he wondered if she was going to swap him for a dog, but then she was speaking again and he needed to concentrate. Now she had reached the bit about a boat trip from the harbour and he was listening intently, wondering where all this was leading.

'When I was in the boat, things looked different, because it was a different perspective and I realised how important that was.'

So, he thought, she's having different ideas, possibly second thoughts about us, and with a sinking heart he wondered if he'd have to fight for her all over again or was this the time to give up, call it a day?

He suddenly realised what was different about her face - her nose was sunburnt.

Then the boat trip was over and she was back in the cafe. He was pleased to note that she was eating, as he had come to realise that her appetite, or lack of it, was a very good indicator of her emotional state. But she was now telling him that this had been her last opportunity to think things through and find the answers and he began to grasp what this day out had been for; she was using the time to reflect, sort out her thoughts and feelings, and find whatever answers she was seeking to questions he could only guess at. He wasn't sure he was going to like the final part of the story and, had that feeling of being in a play, both as spectator and actor.

'And then, as I was sitting in the cafe, it all fell into place, the final bit that I had been searching for and I realised that Lucy was the key.'

'Lucy!'

The word exploded from his lips because of all the names she might have conjured up as holding the key, he had never expected it would be Lucy.

'I thought Lucy was just a rather silly young girl,' he ventured uneasily.

'Yes, yes, she was, but she was also the key.'

If Lucy was the key, he didn't have a clue what was going on any more. Surely Gabriella couldn't have imagined there was anything between him and Lucy? He felt despair wrapping itself around his heart.

'You see, Lucy taught me such a valuable lesson.'

He just sat and waited for the next bit and became more and more amazed as she spoke.

'Lucy had seen in you something that she wanted, and she wasn't going to let anything stop her or get in her way. She just went for it one hundred and ten per cent, all out total commitment to getting what she was after. And I thought, why don't I do that? You've been so patient, Tom, you've let me take all the time I wanted, and I've been slowly testing out my feelings every step of the way. But now I know it's not necessary. If I want something, then I must commit to it, just like Lucy did, and I must take a calculated risk. I saw things from a different perspective on the boat and Lucy showed me a different perspective as well. Both those things made me see and understand how very, very much I love you and I haven't done enough to show you that.'

She sprang up, walked across and hauled him to his feet. Then she slid her arms around his neck.

'Tom, my darling Tom, I love you so much and from now on I'm going to show you how much.'

She kissed him and he tasted the salt on her lips and skin, but also tasted a delirious outpouring of passion that she had never shown him before. They stood, motionless and quiet for a few moments, both taking in just what this meant.

'Darling girl, thank you. Thank you for loving me. I promised you it would be fabulous and it will be.'

Still in a state of semi-shock he looked at her and touched her nose.

'So, my lovely, sunburnt one, as you have all the answers to the questions, what now?'

She looked at him for a moment, took his hand and kissed his fingertips. He had never seen her like this, so alive, so buzzing. Her face broke into a little smile.

'I'll tell you what now and what I would really like, if I may. I'd like a shower; I'm salty and sand-blown.'

'I know about the salt,' he grinned, 'and am happy to search for any hidden sand; but of course you can have a shower, you know where the bathroom is. But, before you go, I need to taste those lips again. I'm beginning to like the flavour!'

'You make me sound like a bag of crisps.'

But she was there, in his arms and it was incredible. She was now smiling broadly at him.

'Would you also do something please? I came in at such a pace that I don't think I locked my car. The keys are on the hall table. Could you check it, but also bring in my sports bag from the boot? Thanks.'

'Your sports bag?'

He couldn't think why.

'You're not thinking of playing tennis are you?'

Her expression told him that something was going on, but he hadn't the faintest idea what. She laughed.

'No and you can leave the rackets in the car. I need my bag because I always have some clean underwear in it and,' she was looking at him now, eyes sparkling, ' I shall need that tomorrow morning, if you're going to let me stay the night that is.'

'Stay the night?'

Had he heard that correctly?

'Yes, yes, of course, oh, yes.'

His voice was doing a funny sort of yelping sound. Totally amazed, bells ringing in his head… This was just… He couldn't really believe… This is what he had…

'Good.'

She looked so calm, obviously loving every minute of his shock.

'I'll expect you to be in bed by the time I've finished in the bathroom then.'

And she was gone. He heard her running upstairs and the bathroom door closing.

He snatched up the keys, thinking what he needed to do next, was back in with the bag: lock up, tidy up outside. He sprinted out and retrieved his notes and glass. Glass in dishwasher, switch on. Anything else down here? Lights. Now, get upstairs. Oh, look in the en suite cabinet. Go, go, go. He did the stairs two at a time, pulling off clothes as he went. Time for a shower himself? He could hear water still running in the bathroom. Yes. He stood under the water for a few seconds, towelled himself semi-dry and walked back into his bedroom, looking round anxiously. It was reasonable; Mrs Mac had been in on Thursday, great. Don't be stupid, she won't be looking at the decor. He drew the curtains, though it was still light, and slipped into his bed, a bed he had never shared with anyone yet. This was what he had hoped for, tried to work towards and in typical Gabriella fashion, she had totally upstaged him. Hearing the bathroom door open, he leaned back on the pillows, heart thumping and then she appeared in the doorway, wrapped in a bath towel. Before he could speak, she had put her finger to her lips.

'Watch.'

She walked across the room, turned her back and slowly let the towel drop.

'My nude, blonde girl, he whispered hoarsely, wondering what was happening to his vocal chords, 'and even with red toenails.'

'Quite by chance, yes,' she laughed.

'Now, may I get in to bed with you, Tom Scotford?'

He flipped the corner of the duvet back and when he felt her silky, clean, perfumed body he just couldn't believe that life could get any better. He kissed her, bit her shoulder, and explored the body that had been held back, reserved, for the last so many months.

'Ooh. Byzantine Shade. And oh, you are so, so beautiful.'

They were both lost in a world of spinning ecstasy; kissing, exploring, kissing, wanting more and more of each other. Then she stroked her hand down the side of his face and looked at him with one of her mischievous expressions.

'Do you remember what you told me about your fantasy in Rome?'

She was now stroking her fingers down his flank and it felt like the touch of a butterfly.

'You told me that when we made love, it would be wonderful. Perfection even.'

'Oh, did I? Well. No pressure then!'

He settled her body a little more comfortably.

'If you're worried, Tom.'

He could just see the wonderful look on her face, teasing, but full of love.

'If you're worried, you could always take the advice about serving aces you once gave me.'

This was so Gabriella that they both started to giggle.

'And what on earth was that? And why might it be useful now?'

'You told me that if I wanted to serve aces, I had to think about technique, power and placement. Sounds useful don't you think?'

'Gabriella Devonshire, you're a very naughty girl. And I'm just going to show you what happens to very naughty girls.'

'Oh, good.'

'Oh... Ooh... OOOOH.'

'Yes. Yes. YES!'

Stupendous fireworks, he thought, as he caught his heaving, rasping breath.

When they were finally lying quietly, he moved a curl of damp hair back from her cheek and kissed her closed eyelids.

'Gabriella.'

'Mmm?'

'Was...was that alright?'

'Ace, my darling Tom, absolutely ace.'

CHAPTER 13

Simon had just finished a twelve hour shift and was ready to relax, have his coffee and a brief look through some post. Recognising his sister's writing on the envelope of one of the Christmas cards in the pile, he slit it open to reveal a picture of drunken reindeer with an upturned sleigh, very much Sam's sense of humour and he smiled. Inside the card were a photo and a letter. He picked up the photo and looked at the group of people, immediately recognising Sam, wearing a deep blue, fur-trimmed coat and a rather strange feathery thing stuck on the side of her head. The rest of the group were all similarly dressed in smart clothes.

But it was the bride who really captured his attention, because although he had always thought Gabriella was beautiful, she now looked absolutely stunning. He wasn't much good at ladies' fashion, but he thought she looked like a mediaeval princess. Her white gown had long, trumpet-shaped sleeves and the top half was encrusted with what looked to him like ice crystals, but he suspected were probably beads. The effect was completed by a narrow band of the same crystals and tiny rosebuds which was circling her forehead and holding back her blonde hair. Whoever had taken the photo had caught her smiling up into Tom's face and she looked so beautiful and so radiantly happy. He continued to look at the photo while he sipped his coffee and then turned to the letter.

Dear Si,

Happy Christmas, because you'll have gone by the time it comes. Hope the new job goes well – it'll certainly be warmer in West Africa than Aberdeen!!!

Thought you might like to see this. Fabulous winter wedding, clear but cold day. Total surprise to us as we haven't been at the club for months. Also gather they had kept the romance secret all through the summer – Alice evidently rather miffed not to

have been in the know!! Clever folks, I say. Excellent reception,
<u>Bollinger</u> champagne and Tom had arranged transport so
everyone could drink! They're going to live in Tom's house.

Brian's Dad much better and talking about going into
sheltered accommodation –possibly a wise move as the other
good news is that you're going to be an uncle!!!!

Write when you get there with contact details. Safe journey.

Love,

Sam+1 and Brian

Slipping the letter inside the card, he looked at the photo again and, as he did so, started to laugh quietly. It had just struck him that, on a summer evening, he had asked this girl whether she would start to go out with him. Not only did he understand more fully now why she had refused, he remembered that Tom had also been in the clubhouse at the same time. Ah, well, some you win and some others do.

Then he put the card and photo back in the envelope and raised his coffee mug in his hand.

'All best wishes to the gorgeous Gabriella and the very lucky Tom.'